Paradise Found

ANIPE STEEVEN KING VPJ

BLUEROSE PUBLISHERS
U.K.

Copyright © Anipe Steeven King VPJ 2024

All rights reserved by author. No part of this publication may be reproduced, stored in a retrieval system or transmitted in any form or by any means, electronic, mechanical, photocopying, recording or otherwise, without the prior permission of the author. Although every precaution has been taken to verify the accuracy of the information contained herein, the publisher assumes no responsibility for any errors or omissions. No liability is assumed for damages that may result from the use of information contained within.

BlueRose Publishers takes no responsibility for any damages, losses, or liabilities that may arise from the use or misuse of the information, products, or services provided in this publication.

For permissions requests or inquiries regarding this publication, please contact:

BLUEROSE PUBLISHERS
www.BlueRoseONE.com
info@bluerosepublishers.com
+4407342408967

ISBN: 978-93-6452-048-5

Cover design: Daksh
Typesetting: Tanya Raj Upadhyay

First Edition: October 2024

Dedicated to "Triune God of the Bible"

CONTENTS

INTRODUCTION 1

CHAPTER -1 CREATION: MAN AND WOMAN 4
   SATAN'S JEALOUSY 6
   DECEIT OF LUCIFER 7

CHAPTER -2 GARDEN OF EDEN-PARADISE 13
   CREATION-REDEMPTION-JUDGEMENT: FLOW CHART 16
   WHERE MAN WAS MADE FROM THE DUST ? 17
   EDEN WAS A GARDEN 20
   EDEN WAS LIKE EGYPT 23
   FOUR RIVERS OF EDEN 27
   GARDEN WAS MEANT FOR ADAM &EVE 29
   THE GARDEN OF EDEN WAS A GARDEN, NOT A COUNTRY OR CONTINENT 32

CHAPTER -3 PARADISE FOUND 35
   GARDEN OF EDEN –ITS GEOGRAPHY 35
   EUPHRATES IN GARDEN- GREAT RIVER EUPHRATES 36
   DRASTIC CHANGES OCCURRED DURING FLOOD 37
   PARADISE LOST : THE FIRST MAN & WOMAN LOST THEIR STATE 37

CHAPTER-4 OPERATION –FLOOD 43
- PARADISE LOST-FALLEN ANGELS 43
- SATAN'S PRIDE 50
- SONS OF GOD..54
- WHY NOT SETHS LINEAGE ?..................................55
- HOW THE NEPHILIM WIPED OUT FROM THE EARTH?..62
- WHAT IS TECTONIC PLATE MOVEMENT?...........66
- WAS THE FLOOD GLOBAL?....................................68

CHAPTER -5 LORD GOD –TRAMPLED ENEMY ...70
- CARCASS FORMED UPON THE EARTH.................72
- WHERE WAS HAVILAH ? 78
- EZEKIELS PROPHECY---DELUGE: SATAN'S FALL..81
- EDEN COMFORTED..81
- 'CARCASS' GOT THE PRESENT SHAPE AFTER THE FIRE ON SODOM & GOMORRAH 84

CHAPTER-6 DELIGHTFUL: DEVASTED 89
- CROSS: WORDLY PERCEPTIVE..............................90
- CROSS: GODLY PERCEPTIVE 91
- EDEN RELEASED FROM SHEOL.............................94

CHAPTER -7 PARADISE RECOVERED....................96
- MISSION OF THE SON OF GOD...............................96
- JESUS PROMISED MANSION TO THE CHURCH ...98
- JESUS PREACHING ABOUT KINGDOM OF GOD 100

CHAPTER-8 DEAD SEA: DOOR OPENED 101
FLOOD WATERS ENTERS THROUGH EDEN REGION 101
CONTINENTAL DRIFT 102
DUE TO CONTINENTAL DRIFT, THE TECTONIC PLATES BEGAN THEIR DESTINY IMMEDIATELY AFTER FLOOD WITH CONSTANT SPEED. 103
HOW THE ANIMALS AND HUMAN BEINGS EXISTED ON FAR MOST CONTINENTS? 103
"THE BOTTOM LINE IS THAT EVERYTHING IS POSSIBLE WITH GOD" 105
THAT WAS THE REASON WHY WHEN COLUMBUS, OR VASCO DA GAMA, DISCOVERED NEW CONTINENTS, THERE WERE TRIBES ALREADY EXISTING THERE. 105
DEAD SEA GEOGRAPHY: EXISTENCE 105

CHAPTER -9 PARADISE RESTORED 114
LAST ADAM RESTORED PARADISE 114
JESUS USED A GARDEN TO PREPARE HIMSELF FOR RESTORATION 115

CHAPTER -10 PARADISE REVEALED 120
DID JESUS MENTION PARADISE IN HIS TEACHINGS? 120

TESTIMONY 134
BIBLIOGRAPHY 142
ACKNOWLEDGMENTS 143
BOOKS PUBLISHED 144

EYE OF THE SAHARA @ PLATE TECTONICS.....144
JOSHUA'S LONG DAY @ AMERICAN TECTONIC PLATE MOVEMENTS 145

PF ENDORSEMENTS 147

INTRODUCTION

Our God is a God of plan and purpose. Brought up in a Christian family, my curiosity about the Bible and its stories increased because my father came from a Hindu family. From my childhood, I read the Bible stories in an enthusiastic way and meditated on them on a regular basis after my salvation in 1982. I understood that the Bible was a treasure of mysteries. God helped me to read the Bible in a year by using the *'Bible Pathway Devotional Guide'* continuously for 14 years.

"For wheresoever the carcass is, there will the eagles be gathered together" (Mathew 24:28, KJV).

"But thou art cast out of thy grave like an abominable branch, and as the raiment of those that are slain, thrust through with a sword, that go down to the stones of the pit; as a carcass trodden under foot" (Isaiah 14:19, KJV)

I often wondered if Jesus Christ used that sentence in Mathew 24:28 while prophesying about the end-time signs. Isaiah was prophesying about Lucifer in the above scripture, and now I realize it gives great insight about the place where the Garden of Eden was situated.

We know that Adam was not made in the Garden, but he was made outside----west of the Garden of Eden---and God brought him to the Garden. So that place should be a prominent place where the triune God came and made man from the dust of the ground. In my studies, I believed that the place should be biblically and historically important place in the Old Testament scriptures. I came to the conclusion that place was Bethel.

Jacob saw a vision at that place when he was on the way to Haran from Beersheba (Genesis 28:10-17). He halted that night and saw a ladder that seemed to reach to heaven, and he said that place was the "gateway of heaven". This word was not used for any other place on the earth and only once the term ladder used in the Bible.

Bethlehem in Jerusalem is the place where the last Adam was born to a virgin, Mary. So Bethel was the place Almighty God landed, and Bethel or Bethlehem was the place where the first Adam was made from the dust. There should be a place to the east of Bethel or Bethlehem where God planted Eden. In the above two verses *carcass* is the key word that reveals the Garden of Eden (present day Dead Sea area).

Hence, "Paradise Found" is a revelation from the Spirit of God. It was not written by mere human wisdom. God gave a privilege to me to reveal this truth to all. " At that time Jesus answered and said, I thank thee, O Father, Lord of Heaven and Earth, because thou hast hid these things from the wise and prudent, and hast revealed them unto babes"(Mathew 11:25, KJV).

As mentioned in the above scripture, Isaiah 14:19, the Lord God trampled the fallen spirits into the pit through the Garden of Eden region during the Flood. You will easily understand this revelation though the details given in the graphics and maps to follow. If you find difficulty in your first reading, please go one more round. I believe that the Spirit of god will help you to understand this book. I would love for you to post your opinion about this book. Please pray for my ministry here in India. If you feel it is worthy, please share it in your social groups, church and friends groups. The benefits of this book will reach the unreached in India through LIFE festivals. If you need any information about this, please contact me. May God bless every reader abundantly.

Yours in His for the lost,
Anipe Steeven King Victor Premajyothi
Author, Paradise Found
D. No: 1-3-49/1, Victory Compound
Pension Line
SMALKOT-533440.
Kakinada Dt Andhra Pradesh
INDIA
Email: victorprem.vpc@gmail.com
Mobile: 8074871493

CHAPTER -1

CREATION: Man and Woman

Jehovah, Almighty God, created the entire physical universe for mankind. In the beginning, He created the heavens and the earth. The words heaven (dwelling place of God and angels) and earth (dwelling place of humans) are mentioned, but the details of the galaxies, milky ways, and the information regarding the creation of heaven was not given. God knows to what extent man needs the details of His creation. The information regarding the creation of man and woman are given to some extent. Man was prepared as a clay shell and when the breath of God was blown into him, he became a living soul. When the spirit of God combined with the clay, the intermediate state of the man's creation was formed-the soul. The Bible says that man became a living soul. This ordinary clay was formed into a beautiful body and the soul had its influence in the free-willed beings. The Bible teaches about the soul according to the spirit and the soul according to the flesh. The former is life, and the latter is death. So the soul has its prominent role in the lives of human beings. In the Garden of Eden, this "soulish" world of human beings was influenced by outside temptation, and the free-willed spiritual beings were betrayed.

We know that the mind is a part of the soul of every human being, and this mind has its own influence upon the lives of people. That is the reason why Jesus, when He began His ministry, asked the people to repent "as the kingdom of God is at hand" (Matthew 4:17, ASV). Adam and Eve's minds were influenced by Satan, and they fell from their state of communicating with God because guilt and shame came over them. This very thing was experienced by Lucifer when he fell from heaven. Today, Christians living against the laws of God experience the same feeling. They hide from Him and are filled with condemnation and shame, even though they pretend that they are living with dignity and honor. (The condemnation and shame come from the enemy, not God.)

God created Adam and Eve in His own image. Genesis 1:26, ASV, says, "And God said, Let us make man in our image, after our likeness: and let them have dominion over the fish of the sea, and over the birds of the heavens, and over the cattle, and over all the earth, and over every creeping thing that creepeth upon the earth." The plural form of the Godhead has been used in this verse. The main reason human beings were created on this earth was to be fruitful, multiply, and fill the earth. They should have dominion over every living being on the earth. They should have filled the earth by extending the Garden of Eden. "And God blessed them: and God said unto them, Be fruitful, and multiply, and replenish the earth, and subdue it; and have dominion over the fish of the sea, and over the birds of the heavens, and over every living thing that moveth upon the earth" (Genesis 1:28, ASV). Here, we have to understand the phrase subdue it. There were fallen angels on the earth working against the laws of God. The adversary was using his power to bring disorder on the face of the earth. So God planned man and woman to rule over the earth. Lucifer fell upon the earth due to his jealousy about the second person of the Godhead- God the Son, Jesus Christ.

Satan's Jealousy

Lucifer was created as a spiritual being with much power, along with other archangels like Michael and Gabriel. I believe that these archangels were given the free will to administer over the universe. The Son, the second person of the Godhead, was begotten from the Father and might have taken part in ruling the entire universe along with other archangels. The Son was given greater status and importance over His angels, as He was, and is, a part of the Godhead. God wanted His Son to be king of the entire universe. This made the archangel, Lucifer, extremely jealous. "Thy heart was lifted up because of thy beauty; thou hast corrupted thy wisdom by reason of thy brightness: I have cast thee to the ground; I have laid thee before kings, that they may behold thee" (Ezekiel 28:17, ASV).

Almighty God knew this from the beginning. It was treated as a terrible sin, and Lucifer was allowed to do whatever he wanted in heaven because of free will, even though he used it in the wrong way. When the sin of jealousy entered into his being; he was fallen in God's sight. He made one-third of the angelic beings rebel against God by encouraging them to support his wrong thinking concerning the son of God. Lucifer spread the idea that God's Son was given much majesty and did not deserve it. I believe that this was the original sin that entered into the angelic beings.

Deceit of Lucifer

This deceit was spread among the angelic world and God knowingly allowed it because being the Sons of God (angels), they should not have been deceived by other angels, even archangels, which was a great sin in the spiritual realm. Today, some Christian groups have the same view about the Son and do not believe He is God; however, they should remember that God begot Him and made Him equal to Him, Almighty God.

"For God so loved the world, that he gave his only begotten Son, that whosoever believeth on him should not perish, but have eternal life. For God sent not the Son into the world to judge the world; but that the world should be saved through him. He that believeth on him is not judged: he that believeth not hath been judged already, because he hath not believed on the name of the only begotten Son of God" (John 3:16-18, ASV, underlined for emphasis).

Those who do not believe in God the Son are already judged in the heavenly realm. The judgment of the world has not been initiated, but the above verse was used for the angelic beings who sinned against God by rejecting the Son. The angels who rejected God's will were kept in judicial custody, which Jude wrote about in his epistle in verse 6: "And angels that kept not their own principality, but left their proper habitation, he hath kept in everlasting bonds under darkness unto the judgment of the great day."

According to John's gospel, the meaning of the above verse is, if they failed to believe the Son, then human beings will also be punished in the same way as the rebellious angels under arrest for the Day of Judgment. But the good news is those who believe in the Son, shall not perish, but have everlasting life (John 3:16, ASV). These free-willed archangels thought that the Son was a created being like any other archangel ever created in heaven. But God warned mankind and the entire universe in Isaiah 55:8-9, ASV: "For my thoughts are not your thoughts, neither are your ways my ways, saith Jehovah. For as the heavens are higher than the earth, so are my ways higher than your ways, and my thoughts than your thoughts."

Lucifer was the liar from the beginning and spread the lie about the Son amongst the angelic beings in heaven and trapped them. Many of the angelic beings listened to him and agreed to Lucifer's false view of the Son of the living God. Jesus explained the nature of Satan through His words while rebuking the unbelieving Jews in John 8:44, NASB: "You are of your father the devil, and you want to do the desires of your father. He was a murderer from the beginning, and does not stand in the truth (i.e. Father and Son are co-equal) because there is no truth in him. Whenever he speaks a lie, he speaks from his own nature, for he is a liar and the father of lies"

Do not conform to the idea of the enemy that the Son is lower than the Father. Jesus was the wisdom of God. Many sects in Christianity misinterpret a portion in Proverbs 8:22-23, ASV, which says, "Jehovah possessed me in the beginning of his way, Before his works of old. I was set up from everlasting, from the beginning, Before the earth was." This chapter was written about the great wisdom of God. Generally, we cannot separate His wisdom and His personality, as body and spirit intermingle with each other. Almighty God wants to give us an image of His wisdom; the image was that of Jesus Christ, which is in the same image that man and woman were created. God was Spirit and Love. The Son was the wisdom of God and through that wisdom the entire universe was created; God, the Son, spoke the words in the beginning. The idea that the Son is lower in importance than God is unscriptural and those who believe that lie will partake in the wrath of God along with fallen angels. According to the Gospel of John, we read that without Him nothing was created. The Son literally spoke the blueprint (plan of God the Father) of the entire universe and thus created it.

"The Father loveth the Son, and hath given all things into his hand. He that believeth on the Son hath eternal life; but he that obeyeth not the Son shall not see life, but the wrath of God abideth on him" (John 3:35–36, ASV).

"Father, I desire that they also whom thou hast given me be with me where I am, that they may behold my glory, which thou hast given me: for thou lovedst me before the foundation of the world" (John 17:24, ASV).

Very recently, I read about a temple in Thiruvanthapuram in Kerala, India. An idol was discovered, which was from the deity, Vishnu, a creator (brahma) who came out from the belly button in the form of a flower (padmam). That Brahma was called Anthapadmanabham, which means, "one who came from a flower." This wisdom came to the ancient kings of Kerala, and they devoted their wealth and treasure to that deity. The treasure, preserved in six underground rooms, is valued at millions of dollars. I believe that in ancient times, kings obtained wisdom of the relation between the God of heaven and His only begotten Son, Jesus Christ. He also a creator and they called Him Anathapadmanabham, which means "eternal god who came from a flower." Hindus gave an image and form to Vishnu and Brahma.

"And Paul stood in the midst of the Areopagus, and said, Ye men of Athens, in all things, I perceive that ye are very religious. For as I passed along, and observed the objects of your worship, I found also an altar with this inscription, TO AN UNKNOWN GOD" (Acts 17:22-23, ASV).

From ancient days, man has wanted to know the real God. The people of Athens, Greece, also wanted to know the true God, but they failed. They simply subscribed to an unknown God. I mean that man's philosophy failed to lead man to the real God. In ancient days, the "God unknown" may be correct. But now, the same God has been revealed to mankind through Jesus Christ. We can believe that through the scriptures: "See to it that no one takes you captive through philosophy and empty deception, according to the tradition of men, according to the elementary principles of the world, rather than according to Christ. For in Him all the fullness of Deity dwells in bodily form" (Colossians 2:8-9, NASB). Do not think that Jesus is a lower status than God the Father. That view brought great trouble to the entire universe. That false view made the created archangel the enemy of God-an adversary and Antichrist. Jesus Himself taught that He was subordinate to the Father in order to preach meekness to His disciples. Many times, He said, "my Father and I are One." He rebuked Philip who wanted to see the Father rather than the Son, Jesus Christ.

Man cannot decide or establish the truth of heaven. Jesus said that when you are unable to understand the things of the world, how can you understand that of heaven? Beware of Satan; he is still deceiving the most educated and intelligent people on the earth. When Lucifer thought of the Son as a fellow created being and deceived a third of the angelic world in the heavens, God the Father declared, "For unto us a child is born, unto us a son is given; and the government shall be upon his shoulder: and his name shall be called Wonderful, Counselor, Mighty God, Everlasting Father, Prince of Peace" (Isaiah 9:6, ASV).

It is noteworthy that God uses the terms "mighty God and Everlasting Father," but Lucifer has a limited view of the Son. So God is declaring facts about the Son against the thoughts of the enemy. He declared the truth that the Son was the "Everlasting Father." God announced the incarnation of the Son as the last Adam when the first Adam failed his course of subduing the earth in the Garden of Eden.

CHAPTER - 2

Garden of Eden-Paradise

"How art thou fallen from heaven, O day-star, son of the morning! how art thou cut down to the ground, that didst lay low the nations! And thou saidst in thy heart, I will ascend into heaven, I will exalt my throne above the stars of God; and I will sit upon the mount of congregation, in the uttermost parts of the north; I will ascend above the heights of the clouds; I will make myself like the Most High. Yet thou shalt be brought down to Sheol, to the uttermost parts of the pit. They that see thee shall gaze at thee, they shall consider thee, saying, Is this the man that made the earth to tremble, that did shake kingdoms; that made the world as a wilderness, and overthrew the cities thereof; that let not loose his prisoners to their home? All the kings of the nations, all of them, sleep in glory, every one in his own house. But thou art cast forth away from thy sepulchre like an abominable branch, clothed with the slain, that are thrust through with the sword, that go down to the stones of the pit; as a dead body trodden under foot" (Isaiah 14:12–19, ASV).

Peter wrote that the earth was assembled through the waters. Geologists confirm that the present continents were once packed together and they spread to their present positions due to continental drift.

"For this they willfully forget, that there were heavens from of old, and an earth compacted out of water and amidst water, by the word of God;" (2 Peter 3:5, ASV).

God decided to check out the useless acts of the enemy and his angels upon the face of the earth. He planned a garden upon the earth in order to rule and subdue the domain of Satan. God initiated a system on the earth to oppose the acts of the fallen angels; however, Satan tried and succeeded in creating obstacles to prevent man's dominion on earth by deceiving Eve in the Garden. This doesn't mean that God failed in His plans, even though it seems that Satan succeeded in his efforts in the Garden of Eden. But when we understand the utter defeat of Satan through the cross, we can be aware of the fact that the cross was the alternate plan of God to destroy the works of the devil. Man was a free- willed being, and there was a possibility of winning or losing, so God declared the war between the seed of woman (Jesus Christ) and the devil in Genesis 3:15.

Generally computers work upon the principle of programming, which takes some logical steps in order to get the required results. We know that Adam and Eve were created as free- willed humans. Just as the computer works on the principle of choice or programming, the entire universe was being led by God's eternal plan and purpose. God has His own programming for the creation of the material world and about the spiritual beings upon the earth. The following flow chart about creation, redemption, and judgment will give you a clear idea about the alternate plan of God to restore paradise in case free-willed man failed to subdue the earth from Satan's habitation.

CREATION-REDEMPTION-JUDGEMENT: FLOW CHART

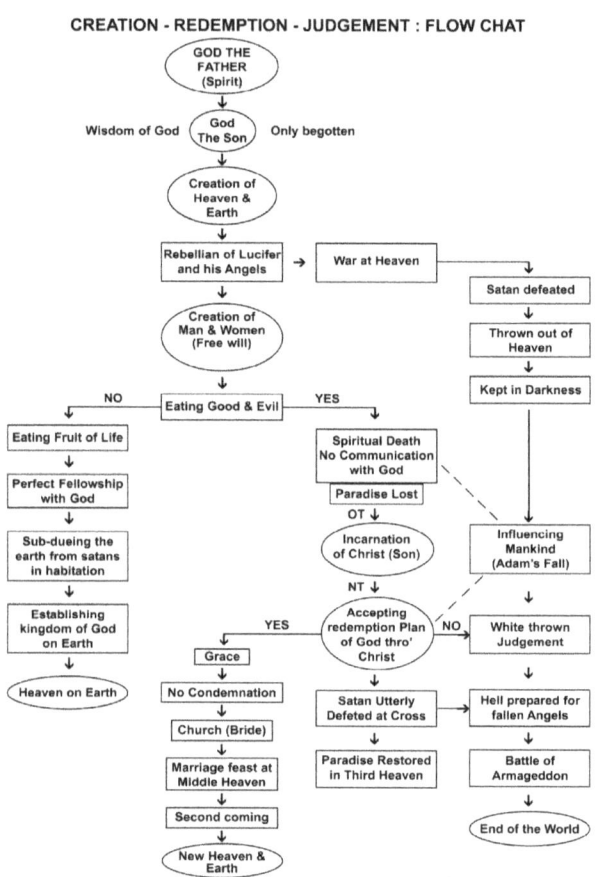

The above scriptures were not about the physical freedom of the Israelites. Jesus did not fight against The Bible clearly teaches us why Jesus came into this world. We always take on the human perception when reading the scriptures, but I believe that the incarnation of Jesus

Christ has a very deep meaning and purpose, which we generally neglect. In the birth and crucifixion of Jesus Christ, according to the scriptures, there was a twofold purpose. Let us see deep into the mission statement and prophecy about Jesus Christ. Roman emperors to release the Jewish people from their rule, but more than that was happening when Jesus was crucified. When Abraham died, he went down to the righteous part of Sheol, which was under the rule of Satan. It was separated by a gulf, as mentioned in the story of rich man and Lazarus. I believe Satan was proud that Abraham was inside the earth for a long time. This captivity was mentioned in Isaiah 14:17, ASV: "that made the world as a wilderness, and overthrew the cities thereof; that let not loose his prisoners to their home?"

I believe that Sheol inside the earth was not the plan of God, but was the result of the disobedience of man. (How Jesus transferred Sheol to middle heaven will be explained in the next chapter.) Dear reader, go through the above flow chart once again; it gives us an idea of how paradise was restored. In order to know the location of Paradise (Garden of Eden), let us find the place where God made man from dust.

WHERE MAN WAS MADE FROM THE DUST ?

"And he was afraid, and said, How dreadful is this place! This is none other than the house of God, and this is the gate of heaven. And Jacob rose up early in the morning, and took the stone that he had put under his head, and set it up for a pillar, and poured oil upon the top of it. And he called the name of that place Beth-el, But the name of the city was Luz at the first" (Genesis 28:17-19, ASV).

Bethel was a place in central Palestine, ten miles from Jerusalem on the way to Ai. At the time, Abraham pitched his tent here. After returning from Egypt, he settled in this place and called upon the name of the Lord. Jacob, on his way to Haran from Beersheba, received a vision of angels ascending and descending from heaven here. On his return, Jacob visited this place and God spoke to him. The Ark of the Covenant was kept here for a long time. This landmark was a prominent place from the beginning, and God has had an eye upon this place since ancient times.

The triune God came over to this place to make man in His own image. The angelic communication was rendered to this place as the footprint of the Almighty God. The will of God is still prevailing here even today. Emperors and kingdoms came against Bethel for centuries, but this place has its own significance, and it is a sanctuary of God.

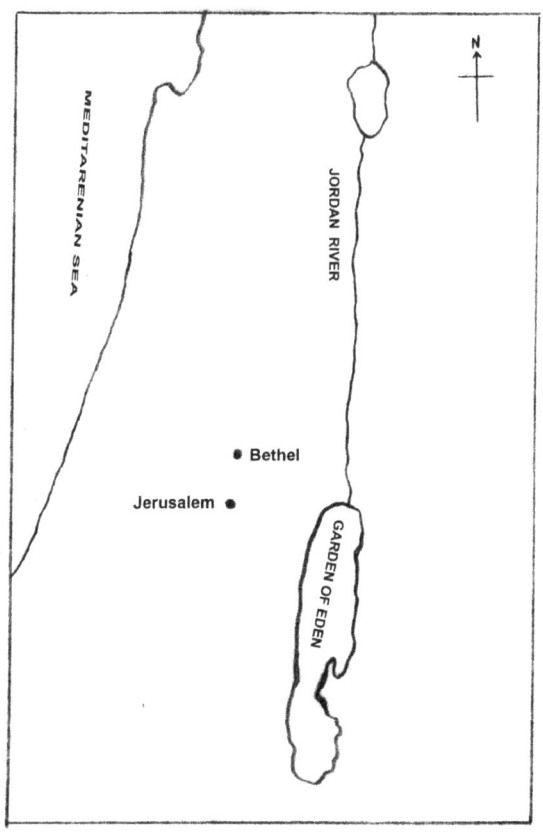

It is represented by Beitin, a village of some 410 inhabitants, which stands east of the road to Nablus. It was wonderful place; Jacob saw a ladder that, in a vision, reached heaven. This was not a common place. God delighted in this place and made Adam from the dust somewhere between Jerusalem and Bethel. God brought Adam and Eve into the Garden of Eden, which was east of Bethel or Jerusalem. I personally believe that the place where man was made from the dust was Bethlehem.

"And God went up from him in the place where he spake with him. And Jacob set up a pillar in the place where he spake with him, a pillar of stone: and he poured out a drink-offering thereon, and poured oil thereon. And Jacob called the name of the place where God spake with him, Beth-el" (Genesis 35:13–15). God had planned to produce twelve tribes through Jacob, and so He spoke a blessing to Jacob. It is written that God went up from the place where He "spake" with him. It is evident that it was an important place in God's sight. This is the place where God planned and made the complicated structure of His beloved human beings in His own image. The Garden of Eden was east of this place.

EDEN WAS A GARDEN

A garden is a planned space set aside for a specific purpose for the cultivation and enjoyment of plants and animals. The most common garden today is known as a residential garden, but the term garden has traditionally been a more general one.

In general, a garden should have a limited space, and initially the Garden was planned for two human beings. The Garden of Eden is described in the Bible as being a place where the first man, Adam, and his wife, Eve, lived after they were created by God (Genesis 2:8). God planned a garden as the dwelling place of the first man and woman who were spiritually active when they were created. Eden is an ancient word, which means "delight." It was an area in the pre-flood world and was the part of the original creation. At its creation, the Garden was beautiful and the perfect Paradise. It was a real place, not mythological. God placed the first human beings there.

There are many questions about the Garden of Eden, such as has it ever been found? I believe we can locate the Garden of Eden, if we search the scriptures carefully. "And Jehovah God formed man of the dust of the ground, and breathed into his nostrils the breath of life; and man became a living soul. And Jehovah God planted a garden eastward, in Eden; and there he put the man whom he had formed. And out of the ground made Jehovah God to grow every tree that is pleasant to the sight, and good for food; the tree of life also in the midst of the garden, and the tree of the knowledge of good and evil" (Genesis 2:8-9, ASV). Let us think about the place that was situated east of where God made Adam. The blueprint of human beings can be taken as follows:

Matter + Spirit of God ⇌ Living Soul

(dust) + (Spirit) ⇌ Spirit covered human)

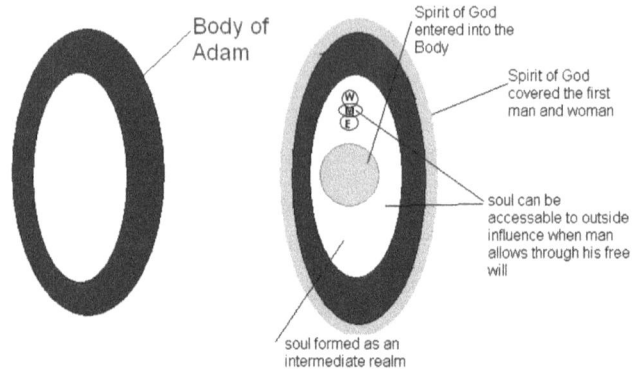

0.3_CREATION OF MAN & WOMEN _CH.02

The Triune God came to this planet by landing on a particular place upon this earth. I believe that place was Bethel. We know that Bethel was very important place biblically. The word ladder was used only one time in the entire Bible, and it described Jacob's vision. God made man from the dust of the ground at Bethlehem, which was west of the Garden of Eden (present-day Dead Sea).

So Bethel was a landmark in the creation of man, just like when American astronauts landed on the surface of the moon in 1969. The Americans who landed on the moon celebrated and planted a pole with the American flag. The Triune God, Creator, came to earth at a particular place that is Bethel. I believe that God took the dust of the ground at Bethlehem to make man.

Genesis 2:15, ASV, says, "And Jehovah God took the man and put him into the Garden of Eden to dress it and to keep it." Let us observe the words dress and keep it. Is it natural to tell many countries with thousands of acres of land to keep it and dress it? Shall the all-knowing God, who is the origin of wisdom, do it? No. The Garden of Eden was planted in a limited space, which was to be dressed by two human beings every day. The present-day Dead Sea region is about 300 square acres in size. Was this area, the Garden, expected to be "kept" by Adam and Eve? I believe that Adam's and Eve's abilities were different before and after the Fall. They were more powerful before the Fall. The animal kingdom obeyed them and feared them. They lived peacefully with all animals. They were no "wild" animals in the Garden of Eden.

EDEN WAS LIKE EGYPT

"Lot looked up and saw that the whole plain of the Jordan was well watered, like the garden of the LORD, like the land of Egypt, toward Zoar. (This was before the LORD destroyed Sodom and Gomorrah)" (Genesis 13:10, NIV underlined for emphasis).

In the above verse, the Jordan plain was compared to Eden and the land of Egypt. The land of Egypt was fertile because of its delta area. The Jordan Valley was also fertile because the floodwaters flowed toward Eden. (This will be explained further in later chapters.)

The Garden of Eden was a place that was planted by God Himself-ordered to come into existence-and full of plants, trees, and was well watered and well cultivated.

This place was compared to the land of Egypt; here the comparison is to the divided tributaries of the Nile and its fertile delta area. In Eden, the Pishon River was divided into four tributaries. The Nile was also mainly divided into four tributaries, but this comparison does not fit with the rivers in the Mesopotamian region. Nowadays, many assume that the Garden of Eden was situated between the rivers Euphrates and Tigris, which are belong to the present-day Iraq and Turkey. But the Genesis account reveals to us that one river was divided into four heads. They have one common source. In ancient Mesopotamia, or present-day modern Iraq, we can find only two rivers. The location of the Garden of Eden in this region was not supported by the biblical account. So the above scriptures reveal that the rivers at the Garden of Eden were like the river Nile, which was divided into four tributaries and reached the Mediterranean Sea. If we observe the tributaries of Egypt, one main river was divided into four parts and it reached the Mediterranean Sea. This area was the fertile delta of the Nile. The rivers of Mesopotamia were not like that. There were only two rivers—Euphrates and Tigris. These rivers started in Turkey and reached to the gulf. But the rivers of the Garden of Eden were mentioned as one river, Pishon, which started in the Garden and divided into four tributaries. We can conclude that the rivers in the Garden of Eden were like the tributaries of the Nile, which are shown in the picture given below. Certainly, we can marvel at the deep meaning of the scriptures.

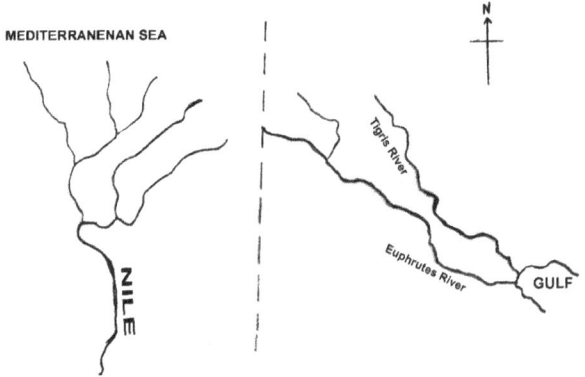

04 & 05 _ NILE AND ITS TRIBUTARIES_CH_02

Just like the division of the Nile in Egypt, the Pishon River started in the Garden of Eden and was parted into four heads. How wonderful are the scriptures? They have deep meaning! We have to understand that the Word of God was inspired by God's Spirit. Paul said in 1 Corinthians 2:10-12, ASV, "But unto us God revealed them through the Spirit: for the Spirit searcheth all things, yea, the deep things of God. For who among men knoweth the things of a man, save the spirit of the man, which is in him? even so the things of God none knoweth, save the Spirit of God. But we received, not the spirit of the world, but the spirit which is from God; that we might know the things that were freely given to us of God."

"And a river went out of Eden to water the garden; and from thence it was parted, and became four heads" (Genesis 2:10, ASV).

In Genesis 13:10, we see two phrases used: "as the garden of the Lord" and "like the land of Egypt." I believe that these words were not only used for comparison's sake but also to reveal

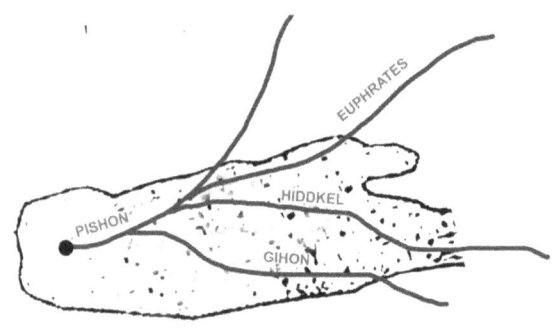

0.6_RIVERS OF EDEN (PRESENT DEAD SEA_CH.02)

06_ Rivers of Eden at Dead Sea. paint_ch.02

the actual location of the Garden of Eden. It was a place of delight and joyful communion of God with His loving created beings.

"And a river went out of Eden to water the garden; and from thence it was parted, and became four heads. The name of the first is Pishon: that is it which compasseth the whole land of Havilah, where there is gold; and the gold of that land is good: there is bdellium and the onyx stone. And the name of the second river is Gihon: the same is it that compasseth the whole land of Cush. And the name of the third river is Hiddekel: that is it which goeth in front of Assyria. And the fourth river is the Euphrates" (Genesis 2:10-14, ASV).

FOUR RIVERS OF EDEN

Pison : It means "the current" or "broad flowing." This river started in the Garden of Eden as broad flowing and encompassed the whole land of Havilah. The land of Havilah was a country in ancient Israel near the gulf region, or Arabia. This first river flowed eastward out of the Garden. The geography of Eden drastically changed in the post-flood arena. So in the beginning, pre-flood, it was not the lowest point on the earth; it was a beautiful place above sea level.**Gihon :** This is one of the 'four heads' of the rivers passed through the Garden of Eden. Meaning of Gihon is 'stream'. The names of the Kush or Asshur are may be the names of the coutries around the dead sea region in pre-flood arena. Gihon not found in the land of ancient Mesopotamia. The author strongly believes that the river

Gihon: This is one of the four heads of the rivers that passed through the Garden of Eden. Gihon means "stream." Kush and Asshur were countries around the Dead Sea region in the pre-flood arena. Gihon was not found in the land of ancient Mesopotamia. I strongly believe that the river Gihon was a stream that possibly broke, or burst, forth in the area of the Dead Sea. Recently geologists have found a fresh water river underneath Israel, which flows parallel to the Jordan River.

Hiddikel : This was another river of the Garden of Eden. I believe that this river is also a part of the Dead Sea. This was not part of Mesopotamia, but the river Hiddikel was mentioned in Daniel 10:4, during Daniel's vision.

Euphrates: This is a Greek word that means "sweet water" or "the stream." The Euphrates is first mentioned in Genesis 2:14 as one of the rivers of Paradise. In the original Hebrew, it is actually named Perath. This was the name of two different rivers, one of which was created by God in the original Paradise and existed up to the time of the worldwide flood. After the Flood, a new river in Mesopotamia was given the same name, possibly by Noah or his descendants.

Some may question how a river can form on a plain without having a catchment area of thousands of acres, which is normally how rivers flow. But it is noteworthy that a great river was discovered under layers of earth in Israel, containing millions of gallons of fresh water. So how does a spring start underground without a source and with great pressure? I believe that fresh water and mineral-rich water bubbled up in the Garden of Eden as Almighty God commanded it to flow. It was said that the trees of the Garden were very high and it was a very pleasant place. We cannot find a place like that in the world today.

GARDEN WAS MEANT FOR ADAM &EVE

God made man from the dust of the ground in His own image, both in spiritual image and physical image, that is, in the likeness of His only begotten Son, Jesus Christ. I believe that God literally took dust from the ground at Bethlehem and made the wonderful creation, man. Why this place? How can we suggest that this was the spot where God made man from the dust? Adam was created to rule over the Garden and ultimately subdue the earth from Satan's habitation. This was the main plan and purpose of God in creating man. God wanted Adam to be the king of the earth. But Adam lost that status and finally Paradise was lost. Let us consider the following scriptures in Genesis 28:12-17, ASV:

And he dreamed. And behold, a ladder set up on the earth, and the top of it reached to heaven. And behold, the angels of God ascending and descending on it. And, behold, Jehovah stood above it, and said, I am Jehovah, the God of Abraham thy father, and the God of Isaac. The land whereon thou liest, to thee will I give it, and to thy seed. And thy seed shall be as the dust of the earth, and thou shalt spread abroad to the west, and to the east, and to the north, and to the south. And in thee and in thy seed shall all the families of the earth be blessed. And, behold, I am with thee, and will keep thee, whithersoever thou goest, and will bring thee again into this land. For I will not leave thee, until I have done that which I have spoken to thee of. And Jacob awaked out of his sleep, and he said, Surely Jehovah is in this place. And I knew it not. And he was afraid, and said, How dreadful is this place! This is none other than the house of God, and this is the gate of heaven.

At Bethel, the angels ascended and descended because it was a place marked by the Creator to create man to rule over the earth. Nowhere in the Bible is the phrase "gateway of heaven" used except concerning Bethel. Generally, the word gate is used to illustrate where we enter a particular place. God chose this place to come to earth to create man and woman. We can also view this as the center of the world.

The present-day Dead Sea, which is the lowest point on earth, was once an upland at the time of creation; it was a plain. Currently, the Dead Sea measures 18 kilometers wide and 67.4 kilometers long. If we imagine it at sea level and 1300 feet above the present elevation, it would be about 20 kilometers wide and 100 kilometers long, including the Sodom and Gomorrah region.

07_GARDEN OF EDEN AREA (PRESENT DEAD SEA BODY PART_CH.02)

We can come to the conclusion that a width of 20 kilometers is sufficient to start a river, which was initiated as a "current" in the Garden of Eden. These rivers were not flood rivers, so the area of the Dead Sea is suggestible for flowing four rivers. Generally, rivers created from floods are wider than the rivers in Eden. The river Pishon started somewhere in this area and parted as four rivers.

Noah's family floated northward in the ark as they started their journey at Havilah, which was assumed to be adjacent to the Garden of Eden. They knew the names of the rivers in the Garden of Eden from their forefathers, and when they saw the river flowing from Turkey to the gulf, they simply named it Euphrates, the same name as the river in the Garden.

Please read this example how Noah's sons named the Euphrates river. We have a town by name 'Kakinada'. But the missionaries who came from Canada into India saw this place and named it "Co-Canada." They saw the actual Canada in North America and when they arrived in this town, because of the common features between these two places, they called it Co-Canada. It became Kakinada. Likewise, the sons of Noah saw the rivers flowing out of the Garden of Eden and they knew the names of those from their forefathers. They most likely called the rivers at Mesopotamia as Euphrates (author's opinion).

Drastic geographical changes occurred at in the Garden of Eden region after the Flood. The rivers that flowed out of the Garden changed their direction. Now, all the rivers around the Dead Sea flow toward it. But in pre-flood time, the Dead Sea area was an upland and the rivers mentioned in Genesis 2 flowed away from the Garden of Eden, the Dead Sea.

The Garden of Eden Was a Garden, Not a Country or Continent

The Garden of Eden was planted by God with a plan and a purpose. Critics may ask why God's plan failed. As I mentioned in the flow chart earlier in this chapter, free-willed created beings have always been at play. God has always had His alternate plan to destroy the enemy, because He knew He was working with free-willed beings. God never fails, but man with his free will failed God and brought destruction and death to themselves and the world. God never took back the free will He gave to man.

Paul said in 1 Corinthians 1:25-29, ASV, "Because the foolishness of God is wiser than men; and the weakness of God is stronger than men. For behold your calling, brethren, that not many wise after the flesh, not many mighty, not many noble, are called: but God chose the foolish things of the world, that he might put to shame them that are wise; and God chose the weak things of the world, that he might put to shame the things that are strong; and the base things of the world, and the things that are despised, did God choose, yea and the things that are not, that he might bring to thought the things that are: that no flesh should glory before God."

God knew the weakness of the dust combined with His Spirit. But God's initial purpose was intended to remove the dominion of Satan upon the earth with His free-willed human beings. After the fall of man, God had to send the Messiah to this earth in order to establish the kingdom of God. At this crucial moment, it may have seemed that God's hand was weak, but nothing could be farther from the truth; God's hand has always been and will always be stronger than the enemy's. We will all soon witness the strength of God. We all should remember that Satan was a created being who is no match for God and whose power is limited. The church was given the authority to oppose the acts of Satan in this world, as God designed the church to be the perfect opponent to Satan and his demons.

"And I also say unto thee, that thou art Peter, and upon this rock I will build my church; and the gates of Hades shall not prevail against it" (Matthew16:18, ASV).

I believe that the failure at the Garden of Eden by humans opened a door to crush the head of Satan on the cross. Man's failure became the triumphant victory over Satan through the Savior, Jesus Christ. It is noteworthy that Bethlehem, Jerusalem, is west of the Garden of Eden (Dead Sea) and is where the Messiah came from.

Israel was named as the Holy Land and God has had an eye on this place from the beginning. Why is this land called the Holy Land when there are so many beautiful places on the earth? It's the Holy Land because this is where our Holy Father came to create man. Our forefather, Abraham, was called from Ur and he pitched his tent in between Bethel and Hai, where the Lord God landed on the earth.

"And he removed from thence unto the mountain on the east of Beth-el, and pitched his tent, having Beth-el on the west, and Ai on the east: and there he builded an altar unto Jehovah, and called upon the name of Jehovah" (Genesis 12:8, ASV).

This is where Abraham built an altar and prayed to the God of heaven and earth. So we can conclude that ancient Babylon, or modern-day Iran, is not likely to be the location of the Garden of Eden. Moreover, there was no biblically significant place; it was farther east to Bethel or Bethlehem.

CHAPTER - 3

PARADISE FOUND

The Hebrew word 'Gan' which was also called 'paradise', means a place of delight." The root word of paradise in Persia is pardes, which indicates a closed area just like a park or "king's garden." Generally, parks and gardens were surrounded by hedges of thorn or walls of stone in ancient days.

GARDEN OF EDEN –ITS GEOGRAPHY

When Adam and Eve sinned against God and gave heed to Satan, God decided to remove every aspect of the Garden from the face of the earth. God removed the rivers and the great trees along with their roots by moving the tectonic plates at the very spot of the Garden of Eden. The Dead Sea is in the junction of two tectonic plates-between the Arabian plate and the African plate. These tectonic plates and their movements can be seen on the Internet.

So it is clear that the Garden of Eden was removed through Noah's Flood and the Dead Sea was formed. Paradise was lost at the exact spot of the present-day Dead Sea. Many incorrectly assume that the Garden of Eden was in present-day Iraq because of the Euphrates River being there.

08_ Garden of eden_ch03

EUPHRATES IN GARDEN- GREAT RIVER EUPHRATES

In Genesis account Euphrates mention as Fourth River not a great river. The Euphrates mentioned in Genesis is different from the river in the Asian region. In the beginning the four rivers flowed in the garden of Eden. But the Euphrates of Mesopotamia mentioned as great river in scriptures flowing through many countries.

"From the wilderness, and this Lebanon, even unto the <u>great river</u>, the river Euphrates, all the land of the Hittites, and unto the great sea toward the going down of the sun, shall be your border." (Josh 1:4) ASV.

Lord God promised Abraham that his descendants will occupy the land upto the great river Euphrates. On the day Lord made a covenant with Abram and said "In that day Jehovah made a covenant with Abram, saying, Unto thy seed have I given this land, from the river of Egypt unto the <u>great river</u>, the river Euphrates:" (Ge 15:18 ASV. Under lined for emphasis)

We knew that as God promised to Abraham, Solomon ruled all the region from Egypt to the river Euphrates but here Euphrates was mentioned as river but not great river that we can observe in the following scriptures." And Solomon ruled over all the kingdoms from the River unto the land of the Philistines, and unto the border of Egypt: they brought tribute, and served Solomon all the days of his life." (I Kings 4:21) ASV

DRASTIC CHANGES OCCURRED DURING FLOOD

It is evident that there might be a drastic change in the geology and topology in the post- flood arena of the Middle East region as well as around the globe as the deluge was global. God is the great geologist, He can make valleys as hills and hills as valleys, as we read in the scriptures. Many geologists believe that many of the mountains that exist today were once valleys. These changes, only possible from God, generally occur through syncline uplift or the up thrust of the layers of the earth. The Dead Sea area was a plain, an upland in pre-flood time, but the land form and its elevations were completely changed in the post-flood world. The rivers of Eden flowed out of Eden and around the land of Havilah in pre-flood times, and the rivers formed during the Flood suddenly flowed toward the Dead Sea (Eden) region after the Flood. If we observe the geological conditions in this region, this becomes quite evident.

Paradise Lost : The First Man & Woman Lost their state

God created Adam and Eve to eliminate Satan's presence, or his useless wanderings, upon the earth. So God gave them great status and ownership of His Garden. God appeared in the Garden when He wanted to fellowship with them. The Bible says man was created a "little lower" than God. We can read this in Psalm 8:3- 6, ASV: "When I consider thy heavens, the work of thy fingers, The moon and the stars, which thou hast ordained; What is man, that thou art mindful of him? And the son of man, that thou visitest him? For thou hast made him but little lower than God, And crownest him with glory and honor. Thou makest him to have dominion over the works of thy hands; Thou hast put all things under his feet:"

God put all things under His foot and gave the Crown of Glory to rule over the earth. Through the sin of Adam and Eve, a curse came to them and ultimately they had to leave their status as kings of all the earth. In Revelation, when an angel wrote to the church, he talked about the one who overcomes. This is the condition in order to regain the "lost" status. "He that hath an ear, let him hear what the Spirit saith to the churches. To him that overcometh, to him will I give to eat of the tree of life, which is in the Paradise of God" (Revelation 2:7, ASV).

They lost the everlasting life

If they had opted to eat of the fruit of the Tree of Life, they would have lived forever. We know that they opted for worldliness and disobedience, so then death came over human beings through them. Through the disobedience of spiritual beings—fallen angels—

everlasting fire was set up in hell for their punishment. This second death is terrible and unimaginable.

How do we come out of this second death by overcoming the Satan? "He that hath an ear, let him hear what the Spirit saith to the churches. He that overcometh shall not be hurt of the second death" (Revelation 2:11, ASV).

"Blessed and holy is he that hath part in the first resurrection: over these the second death hath no power; but they shall be priests of God and of Christ, and shall reign with him a thousand years" (Revelation 20:6, ASV).

They lost their fellowship

God intended to fellowship with His dearest creation—man and woman during the cool of the day. How wonderful it must have been to fellowship with the Almighty God in the Garden of Eden. That was the reason the Garden was called a place of delight.

Jesus Christ cried unto the Father when He lost His fellowship with the Father—when He took over the sins of the world. It was much more painful than losing fellowship with any loved one in this world.

When the believer loses fellowship with the Holy Spirit, he undergoes the same agony and pain in his spirit. David cried to God not to remove the Holy Spirit from him. Many believers today lose their fellowship and run toward materialism and a busy life. Nothing worldly can satisfy the fellowship with the Spirit of God. That was the reason David cried in Psalm 51:11-12, ASV: "Cast me not away from thy presence; And take not thy holy Spirit from me. Restore unto me the joy of thy salvation; And uphold me with a willing spirit."

They lost their dominion

Satan will never be an equal opponent to God Almighty. God does not want to use His power upon the created free-willed spiritual being whose power is limited. God's love toward human beings made Him send His Son, who is co-equal to Him, to conquer Satan. The Son of God willingly came to earth in human form and defeated Satan on the cross. It is believed that Lucifer had fourth place in the heavenly realm, and he had some designated power. He decided to use this power against the will of God to do evil things on earth. God had intended to delegate the power and authority upon the earth to man and woman in order to subdue it from the Satan's habitation, but they lost their dominion. I believe that man's power was not sufficient to fight against Satan, but that's why He knew He had to send His Son-to fight on behalf of His children in order to bring victory upon the earth. The enemy never fights physically. He always tries to induce thoughts against the Son of God (Ephesians 6:11–18).

They lost their home

Eden was a wonderful place; we can find no other place like it on the earth. The fruits were delicious, and there was no contamination of anything there. There were no harmful insects and microorganisms that spoiled their health.

God delighted in coming to fellowship with man and woman. In India, whenever the president or prime minister visits a particular village or place, the cleanliness of the place changes because an honorable person has visited. Like that, God wanted to visit a place on earth—the Garden of Eden. So the rivers, trees, and everything there was special in its nature. Even the gold and other substances in this place, as mentioned in Genesis 2, were precious and today, we find them nowhere on earth. Those things were also removed from the Garden of Eden after the Flood. We are going to regain that paradise in a new earth and heaven as mentioned in Revelation 21:1-5, ASV:

" And I saw a new heaven and a new earth: for the first heaven and the first earth are passed away; and the sea is no more. And I saw the holy city, new Jerusalem, coming down out of heaven of God, made ready as a bride adorned for her husband. And I heard a great voice out of the throne saying, Behold, the tabernacle of God is with men, and he shall dwell with them, and they shall be his peoples, and God himself shall be with them, and be their God: and he shall wipe away every tear from their eyes; and death shall be no more; neither shall there be mourning, nor crying, nor pain, any more: the first things are passed away. And he that sitteth on the throne said, Behold, I make all things new. And he saith, Write: for these words are faithful and true.

The first Adam sinned against God and brought death, which belonged to Satan and the fallen angels. Our righteous God decided to remove the Garden of Eden from the face of the earth, not leaving any single trace of evidence of its existence geographically. According to Genesis chapter 6, the heart of God was saddened that He made man. Then God decided to activate "Operation Flood."

CHAPTER-4

OPERATION –FLOOD

I think the most awesome and most heartbreaking incident of the Bible is in the sixth chapter of Genesis. so loved the world and He wanted His children to obey Him and accomplish His will on the earth to drive out Satan and his angels. But then the first man failed in this plan and went astray. Let us discuss the reasons why a loving God took such a severe stance and decided to wipe out human beings, except for Noah's family.

PARADISE LOST-FALLEN ANGELS

In 1667, John Milton bestowed his great masterpiece, Paradise Lost, upon the world. He mentioned Satan's secret entrance to the Garden paradise and Satan's jealousy towards the Son of God. Milton narrated very clearly the incidents that happened in the heavenly realm and in the earthly realm, and how they affected the Garden of Eden.

Let us read the summary of the poem Paradise Lost by John Milton (Sic):

2 * "Paradise Lost—A Simplified Summary, Book by Book." Paradise Lost Study Guide. New Arts Library. 1999, All Rights Reserved,

http://www.paradiselost.org/novel.html; Internet accessed 15 August 2011.

BOOK I

A brief introduction mentions the fall of Adam and Eve caused by the serpent, which was Satan, who led the angels in revolt against God and was cast into hell. The scene then opens on Satan lying dazed in the burning lake, with Beelzebub, next in command, beside him. Satan assembles his fallen legions on the shore, where he revives their spirits by his speech. They set to building a palace, called Pandemonium. There the high ranking angels assemble in council.

BOOK II

A debate is held whether or not to attempt recovery of heaven. A third proposal is preferred, concerning an ancient prophecy of another world which was to be created, where the devils may seek to enact their revenge. Satan alone undertakes the voyage to find this world. He encounters Sin and Death, his offspring, guarding hell's gates. Sin unlocks the gate, and Satan embarks on his passage across the great gulf of chaos between heaven and hell, till he sights the new universe floating near the larger globe, which is heaven.

BOOK III

God sees Satan flying towards this world and foretells the success of his evil mission to tempt man. God explains his purpose of grace and mercy toward man, but declares that justice must be met nonetheless. His Son, who sits at his right hand, freely offers to sacrifice himself for man's salvation, causing the angels to celebrate in songs of praise.

Meanwhile Satan alights upon the outer shell of the new creation, where he finds an opening to the universe within. He flies down to the sun, upon which an angel, Uriel, stands guard. Diguised as a cherub, Satan pretends he has come to praise God's new creation, and thereby tricks the angel into showing him the way to man's home.

BOOK IV

Landing atop Mt. Niphates, Satan experiences dissillusionment, but soon proceeds on his evil errand. He easily gains secret entrance to the Garden of Paradise. He wonders at its beauty, and soon comes upon Adam and Eve, who excite great envy in him at their happy state. He overhears them speak of God's commandment that they should not eat the fruit of the Tree of Knowledge of Good and Evil under penalty of death, and thereby plots to cause them to transgress.

Uriel, becoming suspicious, comes to warn Gabriel and his angels, who are guarding the gate of Paradise. That evening, two scouts sent by Gabriel find Satan whispering in the ear of Eve as she sleeps next to her husband. The scouts apprehend and bring Satan to Gabriel who banishes him from Eden.

BOOK V

Next morning, Eve relates to Adam a troublesome dream, and is comforted by him. God sends the angel Raphael to visit the couple to warn them of their enemy. The angel arrives and dines with them, then relates to them the history of Satan's fall: how jealousy against the Son of God led him to incite all those in his charge to rebel against God, and how one angel, Abdiel, resisted and remained faithful to God.

BOOK VI

Raphael continues to relate how Michael was sent to lead the faithful angels into battle against Satan (then called Lucifer) and his army. Wounded and in dissaray, Satan and his powers retreat. During the night they invent weapons resembling cannons. When, in the second day's fight, Michael's angels are confronted with these devilish devices, they become enraged and pull up the very mountains and hurl them at Satan's crew. But the war continues into the third day, when God sends Messiah, his Son, to end the war. Riding forth in his flaming chariot, Messiah drives the rebels out of heaven and down into hell.

BOOK VII

Raphael then relates to Adam how God sent his Son to create a new world and new creatures to fill the place left by the fallen angels. The six days of creation are described.

BOOK VIII

Adam, desiring to extend the pleasurable visit with the angel, relates to Raphael what he remembers of his own creation, his first impressions of the world and its creatures, the Garden of Eden, and his first meeting and marriage to Eve. After repeating his warnings to Adam, the angel departs.

BOOK IX

Satan returns to earth, where he chooses the serpent as his best disguise. Next morning, when Adam and Eve go forth to their gardening tasks, Eve suggests they go in separate directions. With great reservation, Adam finally consents. The serpent finds Eve alone and approaches her. She is surprised to find the creature can speak, and is soon induced by him to eat the fruit of the forbidden tree. Adam is horrified when he finds what she has done, but at length resignes himself to share her fate rather than be left without her, and eats the fruit also. After eating, they are aroused with lust and lay together, then fall to restless sleep. They waken to awareness of their nakedness and shame, and cover themselves with leaves. In their emotional distress, they fall into mutual accusations and blame.

BOOK X

The guardian angels return to heaven, sad for man's failure, and the Son of God descends to earth to judge the sinners. Mercifully, he delays their sentence of death many days, during which they may work to regain God's favor. Then, in pity, he clothes them both.

At the gates of hell, Sin and Death sense the success of Satan in this new world. They set out to build a highway over chaos to make future passage to earth easier. Satan meets them on his return voyage to hell, and marvels at the great structure. Upon his arrival in Pandemonium, Satan boasts of his success to the assembly. Instead of applauding him, they can only hiss, for they and he have all been turned into snakes, their punishment from above.

God instructs his angels what changed conditions must prevail in the world, now in fallen state, while on earth, Adam bemoans his miserable condition and the fate of the human race. He harshly rejects Eve's attempt to console him, but she persists and wins his forgiveness. She proposes they commit suicide, but Adam reminds her of God's promise that her seed should wreak vengeance upon the serpent. Moreover, they must seek to make peace with their offended Lord.

BOOK XI

God sends Michael and his band to expel the sinning pair from Paradise, but first to reveal to Adam future events, resulting from his sin. The angel descends to Eden with the news of their expulsion, causing Eve to withdraw in tears. Michael leads Adam up a high hill, where he sets before him in visions what shall happen till the Great Flood.

BOOK XII

Michael continues in prophecy from the flood by degrees to explain who the Seed of woman shall be, the Savior which was promised, who shall redeem mankind. Adam is recomforted by these last revelations and resolves faithful obedience. He descends the hill with Michael and rejoins Eve, who is wakened from gentle sleep, reconfirmed in allegence to her husband. A flaming sword is placed to bar the gates behind them, as Adam and Eve are sent away from Paradise (underlined for emphasis).

Let's look at the pre-flood arena in Genesis 6:1-10, ASV: "And it came to pass, when men began to multiply on the face of the ground, and daughters were born unto them, that the sons of God saw the daughters of men that they were fair; and they took them wives of all that they chose. And Jehovah said, My spirit shall not strive with man for ever, for that he also is flesh: yet shall his days be a hundred and twenty years. The Nephilim were in the earth in those days, and also after that, when the sons of God came unto the daughters of men, and they bare children to them: the same were the mighty men that were of old, the men of renown."

God saw that the wickedness of man was great in the earth, and that the imagination in man's heart was evil. This grieved Him. "And Jehovah said, I will destroy man whom I have created from the face of the ground; both man, and beast, and creeping things, and birds of the heavens; for it repenteth me that I have made them" (Genesis 6:7, ASV). But Noah found favor in God's eyes. Noah was a righteous man and perfect in his generation: Noah walked with God, and Noah begat three sons: Shem, Ham, and Japheth.

"Every living thing on the face of the earth was wiped out; men and animals and the creatures that move along the ground and the birds of the air were wiped from the earth. Only Noah was left, and those with him in the ark" (Genesis 7:23, NIV).

In the above verse the words "wiped out" means everything. The spirits of the Nephilim were gone completely. Here, we can understand His righteousness and His love toward His creation; God always had a remnant to stand with Him to bring about His purposes upon the earth. Noah found grace in the sight of God. The ministry of grace began with Noah and finished at Calvary. It is a wonder to me why many people in India reject this saving grace, as these days are compared to the days of Noah. Jesus Christ mentioned this in Matthew 24:38. Those wicked people rejected the ark in the same way our present generation is rejecting salvation through Jesus Christ because of their pride.

SATAN'S PRIDE

Lucifer, who was once the archangel of light, became filled with jealousy against the Son of God and that attitude led him to incite many angels under his charge to rebel against God. It is said that Lucifer was in fourth place in the heavenly realm and in charge of a large section of angels. He saw the glory of God and the intimacy between God the Father and God the Son in heaven. Lucifer thought that the Son was "created" and equal to the archangels. He wondered why much value and glory was being given to the Son compared to him. "And thou saidst in thy heart, I will ascend into heaven, I will exalt my throne above the stars of God; and I will sit upon the mount of congregation, in the uttermost parts of the north;" (Isaiah 14:13, ASV).

So Lucifer deceived the angels under his charge and made them fall along with him. We can understand his words in the context of tempting Jesus Christ in the Judean wilderness. (It is noteworthy that the Judean wilderness is situated on the west side of the Dead Sea.)

Let us discuss the words of the enemy at the time of temptation:

Then was Jesus led up of the Spirit into the wilderness to be tempted of the devil. And when he had fasted forty days and forty nights, he afterward hungered. And the tempter came and said unto him, If thou art the Son of God, command that these stones become bread. But he answered and said, It is written, Man shall not live by bread alone, but by every word that proceedeth out of the mouth of God.

Then the devil taketh him into the holy city; and he set him on the pinnacle of the temple, and saith unto him, If thou art the Son of God, cast thyself down: for it is written, He shall give his angels charge concerning thee: and, On their hands they shall bear thee up, Lest haply thou dash thy foot against a stone. Jesus said unto him, Again it is written, Thou shalt not make trial of the Lord thy God. Again, the devil taketh him unto an exceeding high mountain, and showeth him all the kingdoms of the world, and the glory of them; and he said unto him, All these things will I give thee, if thou wilt fall down and worship me. Then saith Jesus unto him, Get thee hence, Satan: for it is written, Thou shalt worship the Lord thy God, and him only shalt thou serve. Then the devil leaveth him; and behold, angels came and ministered unto him (Matthew 4:1-11, ASV, underlined for emphasis).

The nature of Lucifer was not changed. He became jealous about the Son of God in heaven. When Jesus came to this world as the everlasting Father and mighty God, Lucifer tried to incite doubt about the Sonship of Jesus (Isaiah 9:6).

Jesus said in Matthew 12:34-35, ASV, "Ye offspring of vipers, how can ye, being evil, speak good things? for out of the abundance of the heart the mouth speaketh. The good man out of his good treasure bringeth forth good things: and the evil man out of his evil treasure bringeth forth evil things." (Underlined for emphasis.)

Lucifer's spirit was filled with thoughts against the Son of God and through jealousy, sin entered into his spirit. Jealousy may be a common sin in earthly realm, but it is not tolerated by God. In the heavenly realm, it was very serious and questioned God's will and plan. From the beginning, these thoughts made Lucifer fall, and it was those very thoughts that filled his spirit, so in scripture, he used the phrase "If thou art the son of God" repeatedly.

In John Milton's narration of the scenes in heaven and at the Garden of Eden in his wonderful poem, a war broke out in heaven, Lucifer lost his glory, and he fell into a corner of hell. The angels Satan deceived were thrown out with him.

This is one idea of how angelic beings may appear:

ANGELIC BEINGS

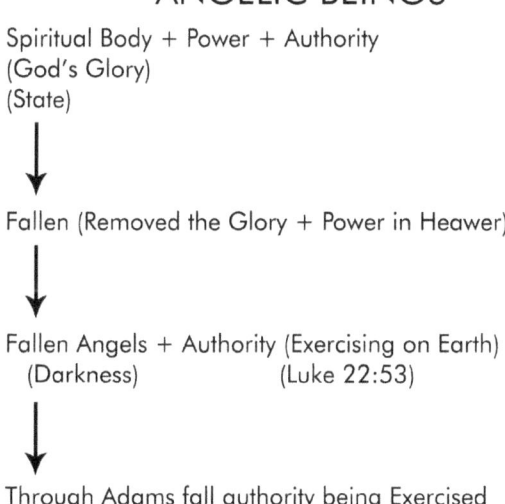

Spiritual Body + Power + Authority
(God's Glory)
(State)

↓

Fallen (Removed the Glory + Power in Heawer)

↓

Fallen Angels + Authority (Exercising on Earth)
 (Darkness)   (Luke 22:53)

↓

Through Adams fall authority being Exercised

SONS OF GOD

Adam was a Son of God. He was deceived and lost his place in the Garden of Eden. He was a sinner and thrown out of God's presence.

In order to understand the concept of the Sons of God, we have to meditate upon the Trinity. We know that God the Father, God the Son, and God the Holy Spirit are equal and eternally the one true God-three in One. It may seem to be difficult to understand in man's sight and in earthly mathematics. But Roman mathematicians gave a symbol for the digit three as III. There are three ones there, but it means a single number, three. God's only begotten Son was made equal to Him as the Word of God. In the entire Bible, Jesus is frequently called the Son of God. Abraham was faithful to God and pleased God, but he was not called the Son of God; he was called a friend of God. Joseph, Daniel, and Enoch were not given the title of Son of God. Adam was given the status as the Son of God before his fall. But when he sinned against God, he lost that status and was driven out of His presence. We observe that Enoch walked with God for 365 years and was not called the Son of God, but he was taken to heaven. So the term "Sons of God" belonged to the heavenly realm, not the earthly realm.

In the book of Job, we read, "Now it came to pass on the day when the sons of God came to present themselves before Jehovah, that Satan also came among them. And Jehovah said unto Satan, Whence comest thou? Then Satan answered Jehovah, and said, From going to and fro in the earth, and from walking up and down in it" (Job 1:6–7, ASV).

Job was called God's servant. According to the book of Job, we can say that from the beginning, angels had the name "Sons of God."

The term "Sons of God" belonged to spiritual beings in heaven, as God is Spirit. The fallen angels were called Sons of God even though they were thrown out of heaven, because the judgment of fallen angels was not yet over. The evil spirits were under judicial custody. According to Jude, they will be judged and punished very soon. Right now, they are in the pit of darkness.

WHY NOT SETHS LINEAGE ?

In Luke 3:38 "… the son of Enos, the son of Enos, the son of Seth, the son of Adam, the son of God." It's necessary to give a lineage to Jesus, who came to this world as the Son of man. It was written that He was treated as the son of Joseph, the carpenter; otherwise, critics or evolutionists may have brought forth another theory of Jesus' incarnation coming to the world as a man. Seth was born in place of Adam's murdered son, Abel.

Genesis 6:1, ASV, says, "And it came to pass, when men began to multiply on the face of the earth, and daughters were born unto them."

Here, we can observe that simply the word men was used instead of the Sons of God. If Seth's lineage was in line with the Sons of God, the usage would be: "And it came to pass, when Sons of God began to multiply on the face of the earth, and daughters were born to Cain..."

The prominent Bible teacher, Dr. Michael Eaton, wrote:

A third view is that this refers to something very mysterious which took place in the world of angels. "Sons of God" refers to angels. This is the view I think is right. The phrase "Sons of God" in Hebrew refers to angels (See Job 1:6; 2:1; 38:7 which refers to time when there were no human beings: Psalm 29:1; 89:6).

This event is mentioned in 1 Peter 3:19-20, 2 Peter 2:4 and Jude 6 where it is interpreted as referring to angels.

It might be asked: can this happen? Can angels marry people? Remember these points:

i) Angels may look like men (Ge 18:2, 8; 19:1, 5).

They may be dressed like men; they may eat and drink. The men of Sodom tried to physically molest angels.

ii) We are dealing with the pre-flood world. Great changes came in the world after the flood, including changes in the angelic world. After the flood a restraint was put upon fallen angels. Matthew 22:30 is true now. It may not have true then

I strongly agree with Michael Eaton that the "Sons of God" refers to angels. In the Genesis account, many times, the good angels took the form of men, such as in the case of Abraham and visiting Lot's house. It is written: "And the men rose up from

* Dr. Michael Eaton, Preaching Through the Bible Genesis 1-11 (Hadlow, Tonbridge: Sovereign World Trust, 1997), 123 thence, and looked toward Sodom: and Abraham went with them to bring them on the way" (Genesis 18:16, ASV).

The In Genesis 18, three men visited Abraham. I believe that two angels came along with the "Son of God" (Jesus Christ), who spoke to Abraham as Jehovah. Abraham used the word men here, who ate and drank what he prepared. Further on in Lot's account: "But the men put forth their hand, and brought Lot into the house to them, and shut to the door. And they smote the men that were at the door of the house with blindness, both small and great, so that they wearied themselves to find the door" (Genesis 19:10, ASV). Verse 16 says, "But he lingered; and the men laid hold upon his hand, and upon the hand of his wife, and upon the hand of his two daughters, Jehovah being merciful unto him; and they brought him forth, and set him without the city."

So it is clear that angels took the form of man in the pre-flood arena and up to the time of the destruction of Sodom and Gomorrah. There were so many testimonials of the saints getting help from angels in times of trouble. There were many occasions where the Sadhu Sundar Singh, a prominent evangelist in India in the last century, was delivered by God when there was no possibility of help coming from man. How was it possible? By His angels.

At the time of Abraham, if God could find at least ten righteous people in Sodom and Gomorrah, God would have spared the cities. But it was evident that there were not even ten righteous people, and ultimately, they perished.

Our God is a God of unchanging nature in His love toward mankind. It is written in Hebrews that Jesus Christ is the same yesterday, today, and forever. If the idea of Seth's sons was that they were the Sons of God, then some of them should have been righteous in God's sight and He would have spared the world by not sending that terrible deluge. If there were any in the lineage of Seth who lived a godly life, they would have entered Noah's ark along with Noah. There were no people who were called Sons of God. Noah preached for many years to the pre-flood population and prepared the ark before their very eyes. But no one believed the salvation (ark) of God, so they didn't enter into the ark. The Bible says that all men were corrupted in their ways on the earth. Hence it is clear that "Sons of God" are not from the lineage of Seth.

NEPHILIM

Hebrew word Nephilim means "fallen ones," "violent," or "causing to fall." These were the violent tyrants of those days, those who fell upon others. The word may also be derived from a root word signifying "wonder," and hence, "monster" or prodigals. Some claim that Nephilim are extraterrestrials. But there is no evidence of it. Even if there was other life in other galaxies with plants very similar to earth, life could only be there if the Creator had fashioned it with a plan and purpose. If God had done that, and if these beings were going to visit us one day, then God would surely reveal this through scripture. Generally, the name reveals its nature. The name given to the giants reveals the nature of the angels who had fallen from their state.

Jude 6, AKJV, says, "And the angels which kept not their first estate, but left their own habitation, he has reserved in everlasting chains under darkness to the judgment of the great day."

Estate- in spiritual perceptive – being part of glory

Estate (habitation)- physical perceptive-dwelling place at heaven

Estate- State—Spiritual beings under control of God

Fallen means they came down from higher state of spirituality of glory and power.

Man's creation:

Clay shell + breadth of life → Living Soul (Body, Spirit, Soul)

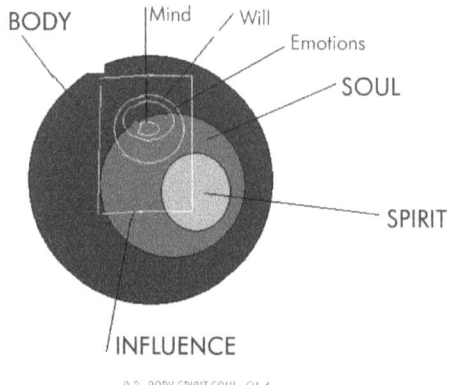

0.9_BODY SPIRIT SOUL_CH-4

We know the process of hybridization where plants and animals acquire a new nature, along with the intersection of parental features from either the plants or animals. This is also true with human beings. When we observe the children in a family, certainly they will have the traits of both parents and sometimes even of the forefathers, which can be explained now by DNA. That was why, at the time Joshua, the descendants of Anak were like Nephilim. "And there we saw the Nephilim, the sons of Anak, who come of the Nephilim: and we were in our own sight as grasshoppers, and so we were in their sight" (Numbers 13:33, ASV).

The last giant 'Goliath ' was killed by the young Jewish boy, David.

Daughters of Men (woman)	+ Angels (man)->	Nephilim or Giants
spirit	fallen spirit	extreme change in behavior, thoughts, and physical structure (giants)
soul	----------	
body	opted a body	

Opted Body: Some fallen angels decided to opt a body in this world. That decision demanded a state that could never be reverted to the previous state or estate of having power in the unseen world. They had to be confirmed to their bodies on earth forever, and the new state was irreversible because they acted against God's will. I believe that they knew this and opted to leave their original estate to take new positions as husbands by taking the daughters of men (maybe both Seth's and Cain's descendants). During Abraham's time, angels took the form of man by the will and purpose of God. But these spirit beings combined with human bodies-spirit and soul of the human beings—and the souls of the progeny, the Nephilim, were totally corrupted, as their parents' intercourse was against natural laws. The imaginations and thought system belonged to the mind, which is a part of the soul.

We know that the soul = mind+ will + emotions. As written in Genesis 6:5, their minds, wills, and emotions were quite different from natural human beings. So God wanted to punish their wicked behavior, as well as the fallen spirits behind them.

A race of great giants started on the earth and their imaginations were quite different from the original men made by God.

Genesis 6:5, AKJV, says, "And God saw that the wickedness of man was great in the earth, and that every imagination of the thoughts of his heart was only evil continually." (Underlined for emphasis.)

It is important to know that their thoughts were always evil. But the descendants of Adam had good and evil in their nature. Abel was good in his behavior, but Cain was evil in his conduct.

But here, the Nephilim race was evil continually. The Hebrew word Nephilim is a term that possibly refers to the nature of their spiritual "parents," the fallen angels. These giants were the monstrous descendants of the demon-possessed men and women whose illicit activities led to God's warning of imminent judgment. The fact that they were also physical giants was later used in connection with the giants in Canaan at the time of Joshua. Numbers 13:33, NIV, says, "We saw the Nephilim there (the descendants of Anak come from the word Nephilim). We seemed like grasshoppers in our own eyes, and we looked the same to them."

How the Nephilim wiped out from the Earth?

Everything is possible with God. God asked, "Is anything too hard for the Lord?" (Genesis 18:14, ESV). And God said, "Also henceforth I am he; there is none who can deliver from my hand; I work, and who can turn it back?" (Isaiah 43:13, ESV).

God intended to wipe out the fallen angels who took over mankind and influenced their behavior. God saw their wickedness. From the scriptures, we can understand that demon-possessed human beings exercised great strength. It is written that giants born to these fallen relations were going against God's will. "Every living thing on the face of the earth was wiped out; men and animals and the creatures that move along the ground and the birds of the air were wiped from the earth. Only Noah was left, and those with him in the ark" (Genesis 7:23, NIV).

I believe that some of the fallen angels opted bodies in this world at their own risk, under the direction of Satan, to work against the will of God and also to destroy the creation of God.

Fallen spirits (with body) + human body → Nephilim (through death) → Demons

(Sons of God) + (woman) = (evil spirits)

Lucifer brought death to the human race. God used the same death punishment to send evil spirits into the pit of hell. Let me explain how it happened. In his fallen state, Satan was then called the god of this world and the god of the air. But dead spirits need a place or a thing to hide or to rest; their first choice is the human body. If that is not possible, they opt for animals or at least images worshiped by the people.

Jesus said in Matthew 12:43, ESV, "When the unclean spirit has gone out of a person, it passes through waterless places seeking rest, but finds none."

According to the above scripture, there was a critical situation raised where the dead spirits had to cling to the dead bodies of the Nephilim and went into the pit of hell while the Garden of Eden was being transferred from the Dead Sea to Sheol inside of the earth. When the tectonic plates of Arabia and Africa gave way by the command of God, it was wide open to swallow the trees of the Garden first and then the dead bodies went inside the earth, and the Bible says that they were wiped out. Ezekiel's prophecy in 31:16-17 supports the idea of entering the trees of Eden and Lebanon into the pit.

From the teachings of Jesus Christ in the above scriptures, we should observe the phrase "waterless places." The evil spirits were very much terrorized by the Flood waters and Jesus was mentioning that in Matthew 12:43. Jesus used a particular word, "waterless places." I believe it was certainly linked with the Flood incident. During the global flood, there was no place to hide or rest, so the evil spirits hung on to the dead bodies of the Nephilim floating on the waters. There was no way for them to touch the ark of Noah, as it was guarded by God's archangels and protected by God's Holy Spirit.

In post-flood history, we also have evidence of the opening up of the earth's surface. We can see that in Psalm 106:17, ASV: "The earth opened and swallowed up Dathan, And covered the company of Abiram." We can also read this historical incident in Numbers 16:30, ASV: "But if Jehovah make a new thing, and the ground open its mouth, and swallow them up, with all that appertain unto them, and they go down alive into Sheol; then ye shall understand that these men have despised Jehovah."

Demons are disembodied Spirits

Guy Duffield and Nathaniel Van Cleave, in their book *Foundations of Pentecostal Theology*, quoted Merrill Unger5** who said:

4 *Guy Duffield and Nathaniel Van Cleave, Foundations of Pentecostal Theology (Los Angeles: L.I.F.E. Bible College, 1983, 1987), 480-482.

5 ** Merrill Unger, *Biblical Demonology: A Study of the Spiritual Forces Behind the Present World Unrest* (Wheaton: Van Kampen Press, 1952), 42-43.

What some believe is taught here is that there was a totally unnatural cohabitation between evil spirit-beings and the women of that day. Those who hold this view believe that this sin is the explanation of why some fallen spirit-beings are confined in chains while others are allowed to go free. Jude speaks of the some who are "reserved in everlasting chains under darkness unto the judgment of the great day." The nature of the sin of which these "angels who kept not their first estate" were guilty is compared to Sodom and Gomorrah where the sexual sins these cities caused the sins of these evil angels as "fornication." So we know these were sins of the flesh. He further describes their deeds as "going after strange flesh," referring, it is believed, to the unnatural relationship between spirits and women. As a result of these great sins, God's wrath was manifest and He sent the Flood in judgment. The bodies of the monstrous offspring of these unions, according to the theory, were destroyed in the Flood and their disembodied spirits became demons. This purports to show why demons desire to enter into human bodies, inasmuch as they have experienced embodiment and are unhappy in their disembodied state.

What is tectonic plate movement?

Let us discuss how tectonic plate movement helps to understand:

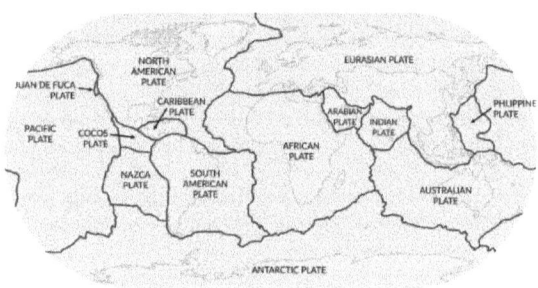

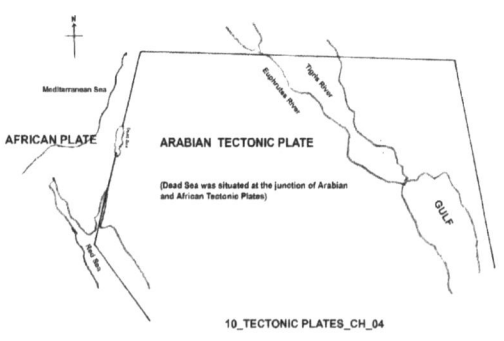

Following are the major tectonic plates of the globe.

1. African plate
2. North American plate
3. South American plate
4. Eurasian plate
5. Arabian plate etc.,

As shown in the picture, the Garden of Eden (the Dead Sea) and the Jordan Valley are at the junction of the Arabian and African plates. During the Flood, the Arabian and African tectonic plates moved apart to give way to the flood waters of the Middle East region along with the dead bodies of the Nephilim. During the process, the "Dead Sea" was formed as a lowest point on the earth. You can view the tectonic plate movement on the Internet. The phrase "wiped out" as used in the Bible explains why this fossil record is missing. Archeologists wondered for centuries why even one fossil record of giants had not been found if the deluge was indeed real. Now we can understand why the fossil record of the giants of the post-flood world is missing. As written in Genesis 7:23, everything was wiped out from the earth while the floodwaters returned to the deep of the earth through the junctions of tectonic plates. I marvel at the wisdom of God; most of the tectonic plate junctions are in oceans, except the Arabian and African plates. These two plates have their junction at the Dead Sea along with the Jordan Valley. (Please see the picture).

Everything is possible with God. He determined that everything that belonged to the Nephilim and mankind was wiped from the face of the earth. Most of the population was limited to the Middle East region at Noah's time. There was a hole or opening formed at about twenty kilometers wide and eighty kilometers long the Dead Sea—and upon the floodwaters a whirlpool formed, which dragged all the dead bodies and their artillery down, as it was mentioned in the book of Ezekiel. (This will be discussed in the next chapters).

WAS THE FLOOD GLOBAL?

Many geologists, teachers, and some preachers think that perhaps the Flood was not global. They believe it was limited to Canaan and the Mesopotamian region. But the Bible does not support that. Today, some Bible scholars still don't agree that the Flood was global. If that were the case, Noah wouldn't have needed to prepare an ark; he would have been told to migrate to another region where the floodwaters would not affect his family. There would have been no need to take all types of animals into the ark. Just as Joseph, Mary's husband, was instructed to go down to Egypt to hide for some time to escape from Herod's plot to kill Jesus, Noah would have been asked to find safety in another place. The Bible says, "And the waters prevailed exceedingly upon the earth; and all the high mountains that were under the whole heaven were covered. Fifteen cubits upward did the waters prevail; and the mountains were covered" (Genesis 7:19-20, ASV).

It is evident that all the mountains were covered. The high peaks of all the high mountains under the heavens were at least fifteen cubits under the water's surface. The geology of the earth does not support the idea of a local flood. Without ambiguity, it is clear that the floodwaters covered the highest mountains of the world. In addition, the floodwaters remained above the mountains for about five months (Genesis 7:18-24, 8:1-5). When the rainwaters entered, the ocean levels would have increased uniformly around the globe. Beings it was such a vast deluge, the floodwaters were globally spread. Subsequently, the level of the floodwaters reduced globally; that's why it took 150 days to clear the floodwater on the earth.

Why were the mountain peaks at least fifteen cubits under the surface of the water? The height of the giants, or Nephilim, may have been the height of Goliath, the giant at the time of David. Goliath was 6.1 cubits (1 Samuel 17:4) and the floodwater spread upon the mountains was 15 cubits in height above the peaks. It is clear that any giant double the height of Goliath who may have reached a mountain peak would die in the great deluge. When God gave an order to nature, it fulfilled His command perfectly and without any deviation, just as the earth continues to rotate in twenty-four hours and travels around the sun in 365 days, perfectly for many thousands of years.

CHAPTER - 5

LORD GOD – TRAMPLED ENEMY

Our God is a merciful God toward the meek, but He will pierce

the wicked. Who can hinder Him? In the fourteenth chapter of Isaiah, the prophet started with this: "For Jehovah will have compassion on Jacob, and will yet choose Israel, and set them in their own land: and the sojourner shall join himself with them, and they shall cleave to the house of Jacob" (Isaiah 14:1, ASV).

Some may think that this portion was written about Babylon. This may be correct, but if we can go into it a little deeper, could it be that the prophet was prophesying about the fall of Satan and how he would be thrown into the pit?

Isaiah 14:9, ESV, says, "Hell from beneath is moved for you to meet you at your coming: it stirs up the dead for you, even all the chief ones of the earth; it has raised up from their thrones all the kings of the nations."

When the fallen angels lost their power by intermarrying with human beings, Satan lost his network, to some extent, to encourage mankind to revolt against God. Now, Satan was literally confined to the pit of hell, but he is working in the minds of people who have not repented and who have not received Jesus as their Lord and Savior. But up to the time of Jesus Christ, he had authority in the entire world, the authority he got from Adam. He actively exercised his authority upon the earth up to the point of crucifixion. The authority of the enemy was utterly removed on the cross and whenever people accept the plan of salvation. Satan's authority has been diminishing steadily as the church has declared its authority in the name of Jesus. The enemy works through a networking of demons by influencing the minds of unbelieving people. The heart of the unbeliever then becomes dark, not accepting the light of the world, Jesus Christ.

Paul wrote: "because that, knowing God, they glorified him not as God, neither gave thanks; but became vain in their reasonings, and their senseless heart was darkened. Professing themselves to be wise, they became fools, and changed the glory of the incorruptible God for the likeness of an image of corruptible man, and of birds, and four-footed beasts, and creeping things" (Romans 1:21-23, ASV).

Isaiah 14:10, ASV, says, "All they shall answer and say unto thee, Art thou also become weak as we? art thou become like unto us?"

During the Flood, Satan lost his power and networking ability to some extent, as some of his followers went into the pit. From the above verse, we can understand that he also went into the pit, just like Pharaoh. Satan was like other kings who entered Sheol (evil compartment) before the Flood and during the Flood. Satan thought that he could do whatever he wanted to do by using the fallen angels, encouraging them to intermarry with human beings. He never thought about being sent into the pit, and he didn't imagine such a big deluge—both were great punishments from God. He wanted to do as he liked upon this earth by revolting against God. Now, Satan has to see his carcass (image) on the earth i.e. the Dead Sea.

CARCASS FORMED UPON THE EARTH

(Only body part formed during flood)

07_GARDEN OF EDEN AREA (PRESENT DEAD SEA BODY PART_CH.02)

Isaiah 14:19, AKJV, says, "But you are cast out of your grave like an abominable branch, and as the raiment of those that are slain, thrust through with a sword, that go down to the stones of the pit; as a carcass trodden under feet" (Underlined for emphasis.)

Here, the above verse dealt with Lucifer, which means "day star," "brilliant star," or "shining one." It also seems to be written about the king of Babylon to express his lost glory. Although the above verse is directed to the earthly king of Babylon, it encompasses a broader meaning of a wicked spirit.

While sending the Garden of Eden to the righteous compartment of Sheol and the dead bodies of Nephilim to the evil part of the pit, an opening formed at the Garden of Eden i.e. the Dead Sea.

A carcass was formed at this region. Note the shape of the Dead Sea in Israel. It is like a dead body wrapped with clothes.

I have seen the carcass of ancient Pharaoh (mummy), and it appears as though Pharaoh's hands are folded and placed on the chest of the dead body. If we observe the shape of the Dead Sea, it looks like the carcass of the Pharaoh. You might be interested to take note of the carcasses of ancient pharaohs and see the similarities with the shape of the Dead Sea. As the scripture reveals to us, God trampled the wicked spirits and the carcass was formed. I believe that the revenge of God upon the enemy was great. Satan and his demons tremble at the thought of Jesus Christ. But too many in this present-day generation don't think much of God and entertain convenient theories in order to continue to ignore God in their lives.

Just remove every obstacle that hinders you from believing the Word of God. His word is eternal and it is true now and forever. Whenever Satan is in the air in

Israel, he will remember his punishment at the time of the Flood.

I believe that during the Flood, God performed the following actions, which achieved many purposes:

i) Sending Sent fallen spirits into the pit of the hell i.e., the dead spirits went to the pit along with dead bodies of the Nephilim

ii) By tectonic plates opening, it forced the entire Garden of Eden-including precious metals and stones, rivers, and trees-to be sent to Sheol, the righteous part

iii) Paradise settled within the earth up to the historical event of Jesus Christ's crucifixion at Calvary (I cannot explain how it was settled and the location inside the earth.)

iv) Many drastic changes have taken place in the earth's geography and the post-flood rivers changed their directions, particularly at the Dead Sea.

v) The cursed earth was baptized in the water and the layers of the cursed earth went into the oceans. vi) In post-flood arena, God blessed Noah and his sons to multiply and a fresh covenant was made with humankind.

vii) God promised that He would not curse the earth any more (Genesis 8:21).

Pre-Flood-Dead Sea Area: Beautiful

The prophet Isaiah prophesied during 739BC-725BC. He mentioned the fall of Lucifer and the formation of a carcass (Dead Sea) as being a one-time event. But actually the formation of the Salt Sea was during the Flood, as you can see in the map of the Dead Sea (without Sodom and Gomorrah). The Dead Sea area was the actual Garden of Eden. The tributaries of the rivers of Eden may have flowed into Arabia in the pre-flood time.

It may be difficult to imagine, but the Dead Sea area used to be the most beautiful place on earth; it was Paradise.

"And he said, My son shall not go down with you; for his brother is dead, and he only is left: if harm befall him by the way in which ye go, then will ye bring down my gray hairs with sorrow to Sheol" (Genesis 42:38, ASV, underlined for emphasis).

"And all his sons and all his daughters rose up to comfort him; but he refused to be comforted; and he said, For I will go down to Sheol to my son mourning. And his father wept for him" (Genesis 37:35, ASV, underlined for emphasis).

"it will come to pass, when he seeth that the lad is not with us, that he will die: and thy servants will bring down the gray hairs of thy servant our father with sorrow to Sheol" (Genesis 44:31, ASV, underlined for emphasis).

Jacob was told by the Spirit of God that Sheol was inside of the earth, which supports the theory of transferring the Garden of Eden to Sheol i.e. Paradise. Note the wording: "go down to Sheol." This oral knowledge of the ancient generations flowed down to the younger generations, explaining about hell and heaven. So according to the scriptures above, Paradise settled inside the earth during the Flood. After Jesus' crucifixion, Paradise was transferred to middle heaven.

Floodwater: Formed Lowest Point on Earth- Dead Sea

As I mentioned in earlier chapters, the floodwaters covered the globe. It would be absurd to think that a flood covering the highest mountains of Mesopotamia or the Middle East region would not affect the rest of the world. It was recorded in Genesis 7:18-24, 8:1-5, ASV, as follows:

And the waters prevailed, and increased greatly upon the earth; and the ark went upon the face of the waters. And the waters prevailed exceedingly upon the earth, and all the high mountains that were under the whole heaven were covered. Fifteen cubits upward did the waters prevail; and the mountains were covered. And all flesh died that moved upon the earth, both birds, and cattle, and beasts, and every creeping thing that creepeth upon the earth, and every man: all in whose nostrils was the breath of the spirit of life, of all that was on the dry land, died. And every living thing was destroyed that was upon the face of the ground, both man, and cattle, and creeping things, and birds of the heavens; and they were destroyed from the earth: and Noah only was left, and they that were with him in the ark. And the waters prevailed upon the earth a hundred and fifty days.

And God remembered Noah, and all the beasts, and all the cattle that were with him in the ark: and God made a wind to pass over the earth, and the waters assuaged; the fountains also of the deep and the windows of heaven were stopped, and the rain from heaven was restrained; and the waters returned from off the earth continually: and after the end of a hundred and fifty days the waters decreased. And the ark rested in the seventh month, on the seventeenth day of the month, upon the mountains of Ararat. And the waters decreased continually until the tenth month: in the tenth month, on the first day of the month, were the tops of the mountains seen.

It is clear that the floodwaters remained on the earth for five months and gradually the level decreased. I don't understand how some people can say that the Flood was not global. How could the oceans in the Mesopotamia area or Middle East area resist the floodwater?

The floodwaters entered into the deep of the earth via inlets through the junctions of various tectonic plates. There are many tectonic plate junctions upon the earth, and they provided a way for the floodwaters to enter.

There may be a change in the surface area of the earth because of the deep ocean basins formed during the Flood. These deep oceans may have accommodated the floodwaters, which were drained from the continents. The tectonic plate movement may have helped this process.

As I mentioned earlier, the Garden of Eden was at the junction of the Arabian and African plates. The tectonic plates opened at the spot where the Garden of Eden was planted. The floodwaters entered into this opening through the Jordan Valley and around the Garden. Due to the heavy flowing floodwaters, soil erosion took place around the Garden of Eden, forming the deepest point on the earth—the Dead Sea. We can see this topography around the Dead Sea by looking at the maps. I marvel at the shape of the Dead Sea, which seems to resemble a dead body (carcass) trodden underfoot as mentioned in Isaiah 14:19.

WHERE WAS HAVILAH ?

The ancient Middle-Eastern maps show that Havilah was east of the Dead Sea and I believe that Noah built the ark in this area. The first river of Eden, Pishon, encompassed the whole land of Havilah. Gold and other substances mentioned in Genesis most likely went into Sheol by the floodwaters. Let us consider some scriptures that mention Havilah.

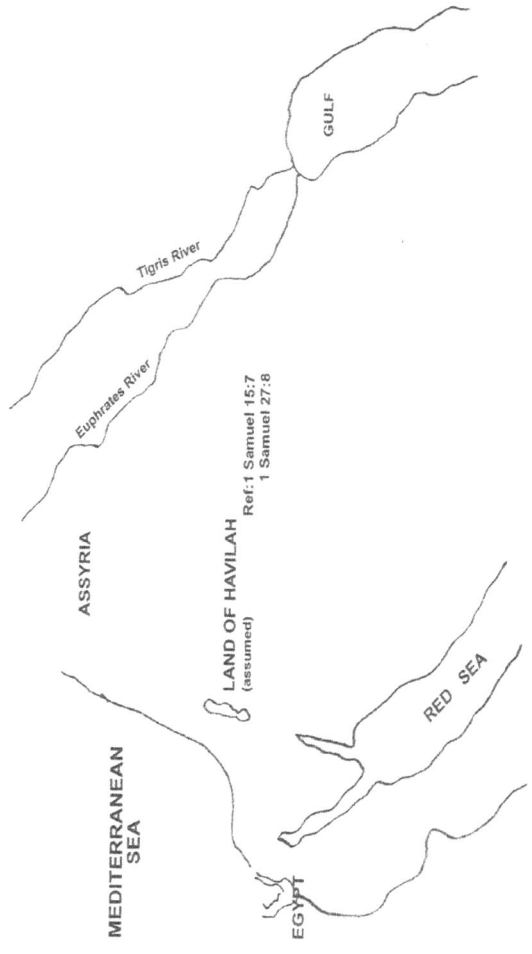

"The name of the first is Pishon: that is it which compasseth the whole land of Havilah, where there is gold;" (Genesis 2:11, ASV). I believe that the first river started in Eden and flowed east, and the land eastward of the Garden of Eden is the present-day Dead Sea.

It is clear that in the following scripture, the land of Havilah was definitely east of Eden, and not as some believe, near the gulf region; that does not coincide with the scriptures: "And they dwelt from Havilah unto Shur that is before Egypt, as thou goest toward Assyria. He abode over against all his brethren" (Genesis 25:18, ASV).

We can observe that in the map below, the area of Havilah fits in a place east of Eden, the present-day Dead Sea. The Shur Desert was southwest of the Dead Sea and Havilah was on the way to Assyria, meaning the east side of the Garden of Eden/Dead Sea. So in other words, Havilah was in between the Dead Sea and the Arabian Gulf.

Remember, the geography of the Dead Sea area completely changed in the post-flood arena. Almighty God wanted to remove every aspect of the Garden of Eden and also every trace of Nephilim on the earth. That was perfectly done by God.

Solomon tried to know every aspect of nature with wisdom given by God, and he came to this conclusion: "This is the end of the matter; all hath been heard: fear God, and keep his commandments; for this is the whole duty of man. For God will bring every work into judgment, with every hidden thing, whether it be good, or whether it be evil" (Ecclesiastes 12:13-14, ASV).

The above verse is a guideline or a warning to anyone who wants to test the creation of God. No man has ever lived in this world who was wiser than Solomon, but you see even he directed mankind toward God and His wisdom. You should do the same. I don't recommend any of conclusions come against the Word of God; it will only bring you judgment. Seek only the origin of wisdom-Jesus Christ.

EZEKIELS PROPHECY---DELUGE: SATAN'S FALL

The prophet Ezekiel prophesied about the king of Egypt, Pharaoh. Generally, prophets prophesy about future events. But here, the prophet narrated a past event, which was a mystery to the people at that time. We should understand that Pharaoh, the king of Tyre, and the king of Babylon are all the parabolic representation of Satan.

The prophet Ezekiel prophesied (Ezekiel 31) and revealed the truth about how Eden disappeared from the face of the earth, and it is still a mystery to mankind.

As written in Isaiah chapter 14, Satan exalted himself. These scriptures have been written symbolically and it might have happened to Pharaoh in the past, but I am concentrating on the other side of God's act at the time of great flood.

EDEN COMFORTED

Sin entered into this delightful place and the trees of the Garden worried about the sin of mankind more than human beings. Almighty God came to visit the Garden every day to talk to His children, making the Garden more delightful through His presence.

Ezekiel records in 31:15-17, ASV, "Thus saith the Lord Jehovah: In the day when he went down to Sheol I caused a mourning: I covered the deep for him, and I restrained the rivers thereof; and the great waters were stayed; and I caused Lebanon to mourn for him, and all the trees of the field fainted for him. I made the nations to shake at the sound of his fall, when I cast him down to Sheol with them that descend into the pit; and all the trees of Eden, the choice and best of Lebanon, all that drink water, were comforted in the nether parts of the earth. They also went down into Sheol with him unto them that are slain by the sword; yea, they that were his arm, that dwelt under his shadow in the midst of the nations.

To whom art thou thus like in glory and in greatness among the trees of Eden? yet shalt thou be brought down with the trees of Eden unto the nether parts of the earth: thou shalt lie in the midst of the uncircumcised, with them that are slain by the sword. This is Pharaoh and all his multitude, saith the Lord Jehovah."

In the above scriptures, a description was written about the Garden of Eden. The four rivers of the Garden made the soil very fertile; the rivers started in the Garden itself. They were not dependent upon the rains or catchments areas. The rivers bubbled and springs came out from the Garden. The Garden was a beautiful place, divinely perfect, and the fruits were delicious; Adam and Eve enjoyed this place very much. As sin entered into this place, God grieved that He made man on the earth (Genesis 6:6). So when God decided to send His lovely children out of Eden, He wanted to remove the Garden from the earth. By sending the great Flood, He implemented His plan of shifting the Garden of Eden (Paradise) to Sheol. God literally did this, and He changed the geographical situations in the Middle East during the Flood. Where the rivers once flowed away from the Garden, their direction reversed toward the Salt Sea due to the geographical changes that occurred during the Flood. I believe that the volcanic belt was activated around the globe with the movement of the tectonic plates during this deluge.

I believe that the volcanic belt activated globally around the Garden of Eden (present-day Dead Sea) was elevated to some extent. The earth opened at the Garden of Eden and the soil, plants, and mud went through that opening. It is clear that if we observe the geography around the Dead Sea, all the small rivers flowed toward it, and fertile soil accumulated at Sodom and Gomorrah, making the valley more fertile at the time of Abraham and Lot.

Why did I use the word comforted to describe Eden? The fossil record reveals that during this Flood, many trees of the world were wiped out and sent to the oceans. These trees were converted into coal mines in different low-lying regions of the world due to the heat inside the earth and the heavy weight during and after the deluge had taken place. I believe that many shores of the pre-flood world were submersed in the floodwaters and the heavy weight and heat inside the earth formed the coal mines. Recently, geologists proved that there is no need for long periods time to form coal. Many riverbeds are sources of oil and natural gases all over the world. Enormous amounts of gas and oil have been found in riverbeds in Kirshna and Godavari, India. The trees and other things along the riverbed may have been deposited during the global deluge.

So the trees of Eden were not buried under the mud and soil; they were transferred to the Sheol of the earth. You may ask, "How did these trees survive inside the earth?" Remember, with God, everything is possible. While narrating the Lazarus and rich man's story, He saw Abraham and cried out to him. How it that possible? We can't understand the characteristics of a soulish body. So it is clear that God preserved the Garden of Eden (Paradise) inside the earth and arrested the fallen spirits in the pit. Our limited knowledge does not explain every aspect of God's acts.

'Carcass' got the Present shape after the fire on Sodom & Gomorrah

"And Lot lifted up his eyes, and beheld all the Plain of the Jordan, that it was well watered every where, before Jehovah destroyed Sodom and Gomorrah, like the garden of Jehovah, like the land of Egypt, as thou goest unto Zoar" (Genesis 13:10, ASV).

We can understand that this area was compared to the Garden of Eden. This was a blessed place by God and a place designed to wage war against Satan. Due to the blessings of God, and fertility brought by the Flood, it made this place lush, and Lot traveled eastward and pitched his tent there. This is clear that the Dead Sea was eastward of the tent of Abraham.

The people of Sodom and Gomorrah enjoyed this fertile land and they had an abundance of everything. Before long, they practiced homosexuality, which was against God's commandments. "There is a way which seemeth right unto a man; But the end thereof are the ways of death" (Proverbs 14:12, ASV).

In their material abundance, they heeded to the evil thoughts of demons and destroyed their bodies against the law of God. This law spoke of man and woman living together, as the first marriage was done in the Garden of Eden, which was very near Sodom and Gomorrah. When man exceeds his limits, our sovereign God will intervene and take the necessary steps. Abraham's intercession was in vain, because the wickedness of the people of Sodom and Gomorrah was too great. "Even as Sodom and Gomorrah, and the cities about them, having in like manner with these given themselves over to fornication and gone after strange flesh, are set forth as an example, suffering the punishment of eternal fire" (Jude 7, ASV).

Now we can understand why our loving God send that type of devastation upon the cities of the valley of

Jordan. Even today, burned white sulfur deposits prevail in that place.

Dear Readers, do not give heed to the evil thoughts of the enemy of God. He doesn't want to go alone to the pit, so and he has been trying to get as many people to go with him as possible. Don't let that be you. I believe the remnants of the white sulfur deposits remain at the Dead Sea as physical evidence to the present generation to not fall into Satan's trap and go with him into the everlasting fire.

"and turning the cities of Sodom and Gomorrah into ashes condemned them with an overthrow, having made them an example unto those that should live ungodly; and delivered righteous Lot, sore distressed by the lascivious life of the wicked" (2 Peter 2:6-7, ASV).

The people of Sodom and Gomorrah tried to molest angels physically, so they deserved the rain of sulfur and brimstone. There would have been many other Sodom and Gomorrah's upon the earth in these last few centuries, but the cross of Christ gives grace to mankind to repent.

"But before they lay down, the men of the city, even the men of Sodom, compassed the house round, both young and old, all the people from every quarter; and they called unto Lot, and said unto him, Where are the men that came in to thee this night? bring them out unto us, that we may know them" (Genesis 19:4–5 ASV).

The wickedness of those cities brought the wrath of God and the "head" of the carcass (Dead Sea) formed. The demons tried to spoil the minds of the people and entire cities completely heeded to the thoughts of Satan. We cannot work against Almighty God and expect to live and prosper. This area was a lively example of God's intervention and what happens when all the people collectively live in pride and without fear of God.

The fire and brimstone rained onto the five cities; rocks and houses burned. A deep bay formed at southern end of the Salt Sea. The salt layers dissolved in that terrible fire and flowed to the Salt Sea. The salinity rapidly increased and the Salt Sea turned into the present-day Dead Sea. It's a wonder to me that many earthquakes took place in this area, but the "carcass" remains, still in the shape of a dead body. When the fire burned the salt and other burned substances were added to it, the Salt Sea became the Dead Sea. With such a high salinity concentration, just about anyone can float on the waters of Dead Sea. This is one of its current novelties for visitors.

So the head added to the body part of the Salt Sea and the complete Dead Sea (dead body) region formed. The prophet Isaiah prophesied as follows: "But thou art cast forth away from thy sepulchre like an abominable branch, clothed with the slain, that are thrust through with the sword, that go down to the stones of the pit; as a dead body trodden under foot" (Isaiah 14:19, ASV, underlined for emphasis).

14_ Dead Sea complete picture_ ch.05

16_DEAD SEA COMPLETE PICTURE

CHAPTER-6

DELIGHTFUL: DEVASTED

When we observe the history of God's people and the kingdoms of Judah and Israel, one thing is clear, man's disobedience and sin made God remove the people from their country, even to the Gentile nations. The kingdoms and great temples were immaterial to God when people lost hope in their Creator and willfully entered into disobedience and sin. God destroyed His dwelling place on earth when the kings and the people fell into sin. History has taught us how wonderfully He brought the Israelites out of Egypt, and when they were disobedient many times, God wanted to wipe out the people. Moses interceded for them and pleaded for God to forgive them. God wanted to consume the Israelites when they disobeyed. "And the LORD said to Moses, 'I have seen this people, and behold, it is a stiff-necked people. Now therefore let me alone, that my wrath may burn hot against them and I may consume them, in order that I may make a great nation of you" (Exodus 32:9-10, ESV).

Creation is not as important to God when compared to human beings, who were created in His own image. Eden was prepared with a great plan, but man's disobedience opened things up to another option-God sending His Son to this world as the second Adam. When Eden was planted, there was plenty of provision and the gold of that land was good; there was also bdellium and the onyx stone (Genesis 2:10).

Now, we can't even see traces of gold, bdellium, or onyx this area. There are just the remnants of devastation.

Do not come to the conclusion that the enemy had the upper hand in disturbing creation by creating devastation and removing the delightfulness of Eden. God had two options that would ultimately destroy the acts of Satan. One was Adam and Eve's dominion in the Garden of Eden, and the second one was the cross; both had the same effect on Satan.

CROSS: WORDLY PERCEPTIVE

Jewish people cried out at the cross, "Come down from the cross then we will believe You as the Messiah." The religious people didn't know the negative impact the cross would have on Satan, and the positive impact it would have on the world. That's why Jesus prayed for God to forgive them and that they didn't know what they were doing. While Satan is utterly suffering in the pit, even today many people in India see the cross in a sympathetic way. They do not understand the seriousness of sin in the sight of God. God's love allowed Him to send His only begotten Son to the earth. The righteousness of Jesus Christ and His shed blood on the cross took care of all of the sins of every believer on earth. Even today, scientists spend millions of dollars to disprove the creation of God by clinging to materialism. Millions of dollars are being spent to discover life in outer space. I believe some part of that budget should help us to reach unreached in the world. They are working hard to prove that the universe self-existed and that human beings came from a "soup," believing that an explosion (Big Bang theory) brought strategically arranged planets into existence. At the same time, the explosion on earth brought disorder and devastation. Man is trying hard to prove that everything self- existed. Manmade theories and data analysis is more important to some people than our heavenly Father. What a pity.

CROSS: GODLY PERCEPTIVE

Immediately after the Fall, God declared His plan: "And I will put enmity between thee and the woman, and between thy seed and her seed: he shall bruise thy head, and thou shalt bruise his heel" (Genesis 3:15, ASV).

Jesus Christ bruised the head of Satan when He was on the cross while Jewish people, in their ignorance, thought that they had finished Him. But through Jesus, God said, "It is finished." That is, the acts of Satan were finished because his head was bruised when Jesus was on the cross. Satan was utterly defeated on the cross. "Whoever makes a practice of sinning is of the devil, for the devil has been sinning from the beginning. The reason the Son of God appeared was to destroy the works of the devil" (1 John 3:8, ESV). Jesus answered to the thief on the cross, "Truly, I say to you, today you will be with me in Paradise" (Luke 23:43, ESV). The cross blessed the repented thief and promised Paradise. He may have been the last one who repented and traveled directly to Paradise. Afterward, saved souls traveled to Paradise in middle heaven.

Paul wrote: "I must go on boasting. Though there is nothing to be gained by it, I will go on to visions and revelations of the Lord. I know a man in Christ who fourteen years ago was caught up to the third heaven-whether in the body or out of the body I do not know, God knows. And I know that this man was caught up into paradise—whether in the body or out of the body I do not know, God knows—and he heard things that cannot be told, which man may not utter" (2 Corinthians 12:1-4, ESV, underlined for emphasis).

Let's look at the phrase, "caught up into Paradise." From this, we can understand that the Paradise at the Dead Sea was transferred to the third heaven at the time of crucifixion.

Now we are promised: "And the God of peace shall bruise Satan under your feet shortly. The grace of our Lord Jesus Christ be with you" (Romans 16:20, ASV).

"And you, being dead through your trespasses and the un circumcision of your flesh, you, I say, did he make alive together with him, having forgiven us all our trespasses; having blotted out the bond written in ordinances that was against us, which was contrary to us: and he hath taken it out that way, nailing it to the cross; having despoiled the principalities and the powers, he made a show of them openly, triumphing over them in it" (Colossians 2:13-15, ASV).

When Jesus died on the cross, the tombs opened and great earthquakes happened. When Satan falsely bound the Old Testament saints in Sheol, in pride he thought Jesus would remain in Sheol along with Abraham and other souls. God had other plans. Jesus came out of Sheol triumphantly and He brought the captives with Him. "and the tombs were opened; and many bodies of the saints that had fallen asleep were raised; and coming forth out of the tombs after his resurrection they entered into the holy city and appeared unto many. Now the centurion, and they that were with him watching Jesus, when they saw the earthquake, and the things that were done, feared exceedingly, saying, Truly this was the Son of God" (Matthew 27:52-54, ASV).

Praise the Lord! This was a public show of triumph over death and Hades. I wonder why many people around the world are still not aware of Jesus' triumph over death and Satan. I feel pity toward those who still depend upon worldly perspective and do not understand the godly perspective of the cross. If you are ready to agree with the godly perspective of the cross, then you will be in restored Paradise.

Paul said, "Wherefore he saith, When he ascended on high, he led captivity captive, And gave gifts unto men.

(Now this, He ascended, what is it but that he also descended into the lower parts of the earth? He that descended is the same also that ascended far above all the heavens, that he might fill all things)

(Ephesians4:8-9, ASV).

EDEN RELEASED FROM SHEOL

I strongly believe that Jesus' crucifixion and His stay the tomb brought many changes in the souls' world. The Old Testament saints, along with Eden, transferred to middle heaven. When Jesus broke the strongholds of Satan in Sheol, the righteous part of Sheol, along with Garden of Eden, come out of the hiding place under the earth. It may have literally occurred in the Dead Sea area, as the Middle East region became dark from noon to three o'clock on Good Friday. There was a great earthquake and the rocks split apart. The tombs opened and many saints were resurrected and appeared to many.

Now from the sixth hour there was darkness over all the land until the ninth hour. And about the ninth hour Jesus cried with a loud voice, saying, Eli, Eli, lama sabachthani? that is, My God, my God, why hast thou forsaken me? And some of them stood there, when they heard it, said, This man calleth Elijah. And straightway one of them ran, and took a sponge, and filled it with vinegar, and put it on a reed, and gave him to drink. And the rest said, Let be; let us see whether Elijah cometh to save him. And Jesus cried again with a loud voice, and yielded up his spirit. And behold, the veil of the temple was rent in two from the top to the bottom; and the earth did quake; and the rocks were rent; and the tombs were opened; and many bodies of the saints that had fallen asleep were raised; and coming forth out of the tombs after his resurrection they entered into the holy city and appeared unto many. Now the centurion, and they that were with him watching Jesus, when they saw the earthquake, and the things that were done, feared exceedingly, saying, truly this was the Son of God (Matthew 27:45–54, ASV).

The Arabian and African tectonic plates gave a way for Paradise to leave the earth through the Dead Sea, as mentioned earlier. I believe the resurrected saints, or the even angels, were not allowed to preach the gospel. God gave this mandate to the New Testament Church to proclaim about Jesus who was crucified, resurrected, and brought many gifts to men.

The earthquakes give us literal evidence of the transfer of Paradise from Sheol to middle heaven. Praise God! Paradise was recovered triumphantly.

CHAPTER - 7

PARADISE RECOVERED

Sometimes we lose things and after some time, we may find them.

shepherd lost his sheep and then found it. It was a joyful occasion. Eden was lost by human beings and then gained by Jesus Christ.

Eden was planted as dwelling place to the human beings with all blessings and sufficient provisions. When sin and disobedience entered into the Garden, mankind lost Paradise. It was a great loss to mankind, never to be physically recovered upon this earth. Eden was a blessed place, having great provision for every need. Moreover, this was a place to have fellowship with the Creator. If they had been obedient to Him, He would have led them to conquer Satan and taught them how to extend the Garden of Eden as a dwelling place for the entire earth. Man failed to fulfill God's mission, but thankfully the Son of God fulfilled that mission.

MISSION OF THE SON OF GOD

"And the scroll of the prophet Isaiah was given to him. He unrolled the scroll and found the place where it was written,

The Spirit of the Lord is upon me, because he has anointed me to proclaim good news to the poor. He has sent me to proclaim liberty to the captives and recovering of sight to the blind, to set at liberty those who are oppressed, to proclaim the year of the Lord's favor" (Luke 4:17–19, ESV).

The above scriptures reveal the mission and purpose of the Lord's incarnation upon this earth. Here, the phrase "release to the captives" is a key phrase in understanding the mission of Jesus Christ. He came to release the "captives" in the righteous part of the Sheol- the righteous Old Testament saints-and brought them to middle heaven. At the same time, He was the Savior of the world. The souls, beginning from Adam all the way to the thief at Calvary, were captives of the king of the abyss, Apollyon: "They have a king over them, the angel of the abyss; his name in Hebrew is Abaddon, and in the Greek he has the name Apollyon" (Revelation 9:11, NASB).

Jesus came to this earth to redeem the present age by a system of salvation and to release the captives free. St. Paul also mentioned this as the triumphant entry into the heavenlies through His cross and sufferings. Jesus took away the captives. "Therefore says, 'When he ascended on high he led a host of captives, and he gave gifts to men'" (In saying, "He ascended," what does it mean but that he had also descended into the lower regions, the earth? He who descended is the one who also ascended far above all the heavens, that he might fill all things.) (Ephesians 4:8-10, ESV).

And in the next verse, it is clear that He went to the abyss and released the souls who were arrested by the king of the abyss. "(Now that he ascended, what is it but that he also descended first into the lower parts of the earth? He that descended is the same also that ascended up far above all heavens, that he might fill all things)" (Ephesians 4:9–10).

JESUS PROMISED MANSION TO THE CHURCH

The first man lost his dwelling place upon the earth, Eden, which was transferred to the third heaven. For this reason, Jesus then came into this world. Jesus preached about a mansion in heaven. When He departed from this world, Jesus promised a mansion. So this lost Paradise will be given to the true believers. "Let not your heart be troubled: believe in God, believe also in me.

In my Father's house are many mansions; if it were not so, I would have told you; for I go to prepare a place for you. And if I go and prepare a place for you, I come again, and will receive you unto myself; that where I am, there ye may be also. And whither I go, ye know the way. Thomas saith unto him, Lord, we know not whither thou goest; how know we the way? Jesus saith unto him, I am the way, and the truth, and the life: no one cometh unto the Father, but by me" (John 14: 1–6, ASV).

The church was promised a dwelling place—a mansion— because of Jesus' sacrifice on the cross. By faith, mankind will enter into this recovered Paradise through Jesus Christ. This concept of a dwelling place in heaven was given through the gospels, epistles, and in Revelation. "He that hath an ear, let him hear what the Spirit saith to the churches. To him that over cometh, to him will I give to eat of the tree of life, which is in the Paradise of God" (Revelation 2:7, ASV).

So as true Christians, heirs of heaven, we should try to expand His kingdom upon the earth and help unbelievers know about a Paradise in heaven. The Good News is the lost Paradise that was recovered through Christ, allowing us to live for an eternity with Him. How wonderful it is being part of this wonderful plan of God! I hope to reach as many as I can through this gospel message of His kingdom in the coming years.

Proverbs says, "The fruit of the righteous is a tree of life; And he that is wise winneth souls. Behold, the righteous shall be recompensed in the earth: How much more the wicked and the sinner!" (Proverbs 11:30-31, ASV).

Every believer should strive to spread the gospel now more than ever before. This is a privilege given by God to the church; I believe even angels wish they could participate in this great ministry.

With our technology, we should pray that God continues to give us insight and inspiration to reach the unreached through TV and village crusades. There is a great opportunity for us to use our talents to expand His eternal kingdom in India.

Jesus Preaching about kingdom of God

Jesus' parables mainly deal with the kingdom of God, which was lost in the Garden of Eden. Through obedience, we can establish the kingdom of God and His principles in our hearts. Godly living has brought us kingdom blessings upon this earth and abundance in the millennial reign. The thirteenth chapter of Matthew is full of parables about the kingdom of heaven. These parables give us great insight, teaching us about the kingdom and its eternal importance. A kingdom mindset on this earth now will be a great blessing in the millennial reign of Jesus Christ. Let us establish His kingdom upon this earth instead of establishing our own kingdoms.

CHAPTER-8

DEAD SEA: DOOR OPENED

Man is exploring outer space by spending billions of dollars, but man has limited practical knowledge about the inner part of the earth. The details regarding the inner part of the earth are limited.

FLOOD WATERS ENTERS THROUGH EDEN REGION

At one time, in a village in India, a river flowed into the village by breaking the bank of the river at a certain point. At that spot, a deep hole formed and that deep hole is evident to the present generations, even though it happened in 1954.

In Genesis 8:2-5, ASV, it says, "the fountains also of the deep and the windows of heaven were stopped, and the rain from heaven was restrained; and the waters returned from off the earth continually: and after the end of a hundred and fifty days the waters decreased. And the ark rested in the seventh month, on the seventeenth day of the month, upon the mountains of Ararat. And the waters decreased continually until the tenth month: in the tenth month, on the first day of the month, were the tops of the mountains seen.

"The The wind may have brought every dead body of the Nephilim into that Eden area, where a hole had formed to drain the floodwaters. I don't think that all the floodwaters went through this small opening. There were many other tectonic plate openings and volcanic openings to receive the floodwaters inside the earth. If we observe the tectonic plates, most of them have their junctions at deep oceans.

CONTINENTAL DRIFT

Geologists discovered that a continental drift took place, moving the continents to their present positions. We don't know the actual time period, but continental drift is real and true on the earth. There may have even been continental and oceanic plate movements after the Flood, while Noah's descendants were spreading upon the earth. It might have taken one day or maybe a thousand years to spread all the plates to their present positions. On the third day of creation, it took "one day" for the land to gather together to form dry land.

"And God said, Let the waters under the heavens be gathered together unto one place, and let the dry land appear: and it was so. And God called the dry land Earth; and the gathering together of the waters called the Seas: and God saw that it was good. And God said, Let the earth put forth grass, herbs yielding seed, and fruit-trees bearing fruit after their kind, wherein is the seed thereof, upon the earth: and it was so. And the earth brought forth grass, herbs yielding seed after their kind, and trees bearing fruit, wherein is the seed thereof, after their kind: and God saw that it was good. And there was evening and there was morning, a third day" (Genesis 1:9–13, ASV).

Due to continental drift, the tectonic plates began their destiny immediately after Flood with constant speed.

HOW THE ANIMALS AND HUMAN BEINGS EXISTED ON FAR MOST CONTINENTS?

After the Flood, the blessings of Almighty God were upon the earth. The curse was removed through the baptism of the earth by the global flood. God made a fresh covenant with Noah. I believe that the birth rate of humans was very high and a population explosion took place. Immediately after the Flood, many people took up the big project of building a tower at Babel. After the tower of Babel incident, generations sought new lands to occupy, as their languages were different and they faced many problems in communicating with each other. They wanted to depart from each other quickly according to their language.

Genesis records: "Come, let us go down, and there confound their language, that they may not understand one another's speech. So Jehovah scattered them abroad from thence upon the face of all the earth: and they left off building the city. Therefore was the name of it called Babel; because Jehovah did there confound the language of all the earth: and from thence did Jehovah scatter them abroad upon the face of all the earth" (Genesis 11:7-9, ASV).

Due to language differences, the descendants of Noah scattered very rapidly to many lands. At that time, the continents were reachable to human beings by foot and with small boats, and the animals with them also occupied these reachable continents.

"As for you, be fruitful and increase in number; multiply on the earth and increase upon it" (Genesis 9:7, NIV). They were quickly dividing according to their language and creed, and they were all in search of new land for their offspring and cattle, because cattle and agriculture was the main source of their livelihood. In post-flood times, the continents were relatively close compared to today. So the descendants of Noah, who were divided according to their language, might have reached continents that were already moving. At that time, the divided language groups were in search of new land masses. This may be how human beings reached the farmost continents like Australia.

There is other evidence from scriptures that the continents divided in the post-flood arena. There was a population explosion that took place by the fresh covenant of God with Noah. This was evident in Genesis 11. They took up a great project of building the tower of Babel in order to reach heaven in their own way, just as some sects today try to reach God in their own way.

Just before the Babel tower incident, it is written that the earth was divided during a man named Peleg's time. "And unto Eber were born two sons: The name of the one was Peleg. For in his days was the earth divided. And his brother's name was Joktan" (Genesis 10:25, ASV). Why was this verse written in the Bible? The continental drift initiated by God at that time, after the Flood, gave the present shape to the earth. We should not compare the rate of present continental drift to the rate of continental drift of the early post-flood arena.

"The bottom line is that everything is possible with God"

That was the reason why when Columbus, or Vasco da Gama, discovered new continents, there were tribes already existing there.

DEAD SEA GEOGRAPHY: EXISTENCE

During the Flood, all the rivers formed around the Dead Sea area flowed toward it, accumulating much mud and a fertile delta in the valley of Jordan. The valley, which Lot saw, was beautiful just like Eden and the fertile land of Egypt.

"And Lot lifted up his eyes, and beheld all the Plain of the Jordan, that it was well watered every where, before Jehovah destroyed Sodom and Gomorrah, like the garden of Jehovah, like the land of Egypt, as thou goest unto Zoar" (Genesis 13:10, ASV).

As I mentioned earlier, the floodwaters from all directions of the Middle East region drained toward the Dead Sea region, and a fertile belt was formed, as shown in the above picture. Lot saw this plain and traveled from Bethel eastward and pitched his tent at Sodom and Gomorrah. Driven by materialism, Lot traveled from the house of God (the Lord's footprint) into the bosom of sin. Dear Readers, never lose sight of how materialism can take hold of man. We can't see spiritual things with our natural eyes. Lot used his natural eyes and went after materialism, and Abraham sought the will of God; he remained in Bethel, which was the dwelling place of God. We know that Abraham was blessed by God in all aspects.

Why Carcasses of Nephilim Were Missed In the Fossil Record

I believe there is a reason why God did not allow us to see the carcasses of the pre-flood wicked people. He doesn't want man to make models of Nephilim, like we do with dinosaurs and all other fossils being discovered in the layers of earth. If these fossil records were available to us, we would have seen images of Nephilim everywhere, and there may have even been people who worshipped these models as ancient gods. Then perhaps Hollywood might have released many movies regarding the lifestyle and actions of those wicked people. God intentionally did not allow the fossil record of Nephilim to remain on earth. The scripture is clear when it says "blotted out." God wanted to remove every bit of evidence of the Nephilim and the Garden of Eden because those two incidents grieved His heart very deeply. "He blotted out every living thing that was on the face of the ground, man and animals and creeping things and birds of the heavens. They were blotted out from the earth. Only Noah was left, and those who were with him in the ark" (Genesis 7:23, ESV).

Generally, when you have something that is spoiled in the house, it is swept away or discarded in some way. Likewise, those things that were not useful to mankind were completely blotted out. God spoke the same through the prophet Isaiah when He was prophesying the fall of Lucifer: "'I will also make it a possession for the porcupine, and pools of water: and I will sweep it with the besom of destruction, saith Jehovah of hosts" (Isaiah 14:23, ASV).

We should observe the word usage in the scriptures. In Genesis 7:23, the phrase "blotted out" was used, which means "to clean out." In Isaiah 14:23, the prophet used the phrase "besom of destruction." In the NASB translation, it reads: "broom of destruction." The global deluge (destruction) was used to blot out the carcasses of Nephilim from the earth.

"For Jehovah of hosts hath purposed, and who shall annul it? and his hand is stretched out, and who shall turn it back?" (Isaiah 14:27, ASV).

God revealed this mystery through the prophet Ezekiel:

Thus saith the Lord Jehovah: In the day when he went down to Sheol I caused a mourning: I covered the deep for him, and I restrained the rivers thereof; and the great waters were stayed; and I caused Lebanon to mourn for him, and all the trees of the field fainted for him. I made the nations to shake at the sound of his fall, when I cast him down to Sheol with them that descend into the pit; and all the trees of Eden, the choice and best of Lebanon, all that drink water, were comforted in the neither parts of the earth. They also went down into Sheol with him unto them that are slain by the sword; yea, they that were his arm, that dwelt under his shadow in the midst of the nations.

To whom art thou thus like in glory and in greatness among the trees of Eden? yet shalt thou be brought down with the trees of Eden unto the nether parts of the earth: thou shalt lie in the midst of the uncircumcised, with them that are slain by the sword. This is Pharaoh and all his multitude, saith the Lord Jehovah" (Ezekiel 31:15–18, ASV).

The above scriptures seem to be a prophecy about Pharaoh, but a mystery was revealed here. God cast Lucifer into the pit along with the dead spirits of Nephilim. Symbolically, Lucifer was compared to Pharaoh in these scriptures. Lucifer was in heaven before his fall. Now he was in the midst of the uncircumcised, i.e. with the dead spirits of Nephilim as recorded in scriptures above.

It is interesting to observe that many idols being worshipped by people were almost black, just like a carcass floating on the waters. Many people today are blinded and ignorant about distinguishing between the light and the darkness of this world. The god of this world, Satan, has blinded the unbelievers so that they do not see light of the gospel of the glory of Christ, who is the image of God. For we preach not about ourselves, but Christ Jesus as Lord. "Light shall shine out of darkness, who shined in our hearts, to give the light of the knowledge of the glory of God in the face of Jesus Christ" (2 Corinthians 4:6, ASV).

John wrote in his gospel: "And the light shineth in the darkness; and the darkness apprehended it not" (John 1:5, ASV).

The Height of Their Pride

God opposed pride and give grace to the meek. The hybrid generation of the pre-flood world was filled with pride and evil thoughts. The prophet Ezekiel narrated the pride of the Nephilim in his prophecy in Ezekiel 31:10-14. People are always trying to work against the Word of God to disprove it. What a terrible thought to oppose the will of God and His salvation. In this grace period, it may be tolerated, but at some point, they will have to submit their explanation at the thrown of God.

Some scientists wonder exactly where the ark of Noah was lifted up onto the floodwaters, and how it actually traveled on the water. I believe that the ark was prepared on the plains of Havilah, which existed east of the Garden of Eden. It was a wonder to me that Noah was not hindered by these wicked people. They mocked Noah and considered him a crazy old man. The ark was built with gopher wood. After the ark was built, there was no other mention in the Bible about gopher wood. Isn't that interesting? The prophecies in Ezekiel give an account of the height of the Nephilim in the pre-flood world.

Therefore thus said the Lord Jehovah: Because thou art exalted in stature, and he hath set his top among the thick boughs, and his heart is lifted up in his height; I will even deliver him into the hand of the mighty one of the nations; he shall surely deal with him; I have driven him out for his wickedness. And strangers, the terrible of the nations, have cut him off, and have left him: upon the mountains and in all the valleys his branches are fallen, and his boughs are broken by all the watercourses of the land; and all the peoples of the earth are gone down from his shadow, and have left him. Upon his ruin all the birds of the heavens shall dwell, and all the beasts of the field shall be upon his branches; to the end that none of all the trees by the waters exalt themselves in their stature, neither set their top among the thick boughs, nor that their mighty ones stand up on their height, even all that drink water: for they are all delivered unto death, to the nether parts of the earth, in the midst of the children of men, with them that go down to the pit.

Thus saith the Lord Jehovah: In the day when he went down to Sheol I caused a mourning: I covered the deep for him, and I restrained the rivers thereof; and the great waters were stayed; and I caused Lebanon to mourn for him, and all the trees of the field fainted for him. I made the nations to shake at the sound of his fall, when I cast him down to Sheol with them that descend into the pit; and all the trees of Eden, the choice and best of Lebanon, all that drink water, were comforted in the nether parts of the earth. They also went down into Sheol with him unto them that are slain by the sword; yea, they that were his arm, that dwelt under his shadow in the midst of the nations. To whom art thou thus like in glory and in greatness among the trees of Eden? yet shalt thou be brought down with the trees of Eden unto the nether parts of the earth: thou shalt lie in the midst of the uncircumcised, with them that are slain by the sword. This is Pharaoh and all his multitude, saith the Lord Jehovah (Ezekiel 31:10-18, ASV, underlined for emphasis).

Noah's Ark sailed north very safely, in spite of all the disturbances under the water. The ark then rested on Mount Ararat in the Mesopotamian region. Noah's sons, Shem, Ham, and Japeth, began to repopulate the earth.

We know that Abraham, who was the descendant of Shem, was brought from Mesopotamia and promised the land that the Israelites occupied during Joshua's time. Through Abraham, Jacob, and then David, Jesus

Christ came into this world and ultimately defeated Satan.

Sinkholes at the Dead Sea Support What?

Why sinkholes are now being formed at the Dead Sea is a challenge to the geologists in Israel. When the tectonic plates closed at the Dead Sea, there may have been some gaps in between the layers of mud and soil. They are re-arranging now and sinkholes are being formed. These re-arrangements occur in oceans, but we don't notice them as clearly as at the Dead Sea. Today in Israel, the issue of sinkholes is regular news.

This is also evidence that the Garden of Eden was wiped out from earth in this area, as many incredible geological changes have taken place in the post-flood arena of the Dead Sea. It was changed into the deepest point on the earth and remains as lively evidence of the great deluge. When huge amounts of waters flow toward a region the upper sedimentary layers go along with the flow. This type of geographical situation prevails at the Dead Sea, and we cannot find this type of topology anywhere else in the world.

Many people are being swallowed by these sinkholes. These sinkholes became an obstacle to building hotels and other projects on the shores of the Dead Sea. There are about 3000 sinkholes formed around the Dead Sea so far. In addition, the water level is sinking at an alarming rate. When the Garden of Eden was removed from its lace, the Dead Sea was formed; however, Eden was safely transferred to Sheol through the global flood, and at the time of Jesus' crucifixion, it was sent to third heaven.

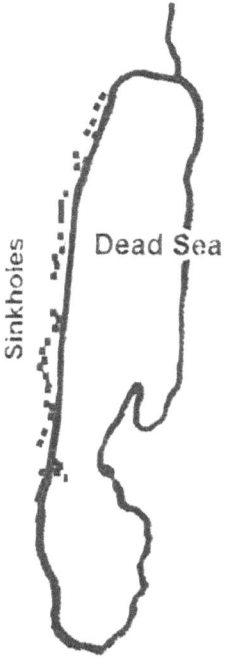

CHAPTER - 9

PARADISE RESTORED

Last Adam restored Paradise

God had a plan to restore Paradise. God has never, and will never, compromise with sin and the enemy. He sent His only begotten Son who defeated the enemy in order to bring the gift of salvation to mankind. Paul said: "So also it is written, The first man Adam became a living soul. The last Adam became a life-giving spirit" (1 Corinthians 15:45, ASV).

The first man was formed from the dust and God breathed the breath of life into his nostrils. Man then became a living soul. The soul of man (mind, will, emotions) is vulnerable to outside temptation. Eve failed to resist the enemy by giving heed to the temptation of Satan i.e. the serpent.

Since the beginning, Satan has tempted in the same ways:

1. Lust of the eye
2. Lust of the flesh
3. The pride of life (I John 2:16)

Satan used these steps to bring the first couple into sin. The last Adam, Jesus Christ, was tempted in the same way in the Judean wilderness, but He was victorious over the enemy and He was ministered to by angels. This wonderful incident was recorded in Matthew 4:1-11. It is interesting to note that Jesus was tempted beside the Garden of Eden (present-day Dead Sea).

Jesus used a Garden to prepare Himself for Restoration

It was recorded in Mark 14:32-36, ASV: "And they come unto a place which was named Gethsemane: and he saith unto his disciples, Sit ye here, while I pray. And he taketh with him Peter and James and John, and began to be greatly amazed, and sore troubled. And he saith unto them, My soul is exceeding sorrowful even unto death: abide ye here, and watch. And he went forward a little, and fell on the ground, and prayed that, if it were possible, the hour might pass away from him. And he said, Abba, Father, all things are possible unto thee; remove this cup from me: howbeit not what I will, but what thou wilt."

The curse came to the Garden of Eden through the first Adam. The last Adam, Jesus Christ, suffered in the Garden of Gethsemane in order to restore Paradise to its designated place. Abraham died and went to righteous part of Sheol and remained there. Satan thought that as Abraham came to Sheol and remained there, Jesus Christ, descendant of Abraham, was also going to remain in Sheol forever. These thought of Satan were disproved and Jesus was resurrected on the third day.

Jesus pleaded with His father and removed the curse upon the Old Testament saints. His agony touched every atom of his body and His sweat literally came out as blood. No man in this world has ever agonized to that extent. As mentioned above in Mark14:36, Jesus prayed to the Father to remove the cup. I believe that was the cup of curse and sin of the world. Jesus knew how sin accumulated upon mankind and that sin mocked Him, persecuted Him, and brought shame to Him upon the cross. He willingly accepted this shameful act of taking the sin of the world as the Lamb of God.

Paul wrote to Timothy in 2 Timothy 2:11-12, ASV: "Faithful is the saying: For if we died with him, we shall also live with him: if we endure, we shall also reign with him: if we shall deny him, he also will deny us:" If we are ready to suffer with Christ, then we will reign with Christ in the future. As God's servant, I have gone through many difficulties and sufferings but my one hope has always been with Jesus Christ, who brought me out victoriously.

The souls of the saints were in Sheol from Adam to the thief on the cross. During Jesus' crucifixion, their souls were released from prison and they all were transferred to Paradise into the third heaven. They are in complete rest in that delightful place. The evil part of Sheol is under curse, darkness, and agony right now without any hope. Dear young men and women, do you want to live eternally with God? Come to Jesus; He will give you a glorious hope and the promise of eternal life with Him in heaven. Dear Reader, come out of materialism and make a decision to receive the plan of salvation. Jesus paid the cost, by which our righteous God was satisfied. If you want enter Paradise by some other way, you may satisfy your soul with your rituals, but you can't reach the Father that way; you will end up in another place. Jesus is only way to heaven, the restored Paradise. Many people in India are deceived, thinking that all ways will reach the Father. There was no scriptural support to that view. In fact, the scripture is very clear on this. "Jesus said to him, 'I am the way, and the truth, and the life; no one come to the Father but through Me" (John 14:6, NASB).

Paradise Boundaries Extended

The area of the Garden of Eden may have been about 300 square acres. The area of the Dead Sea is estimated at about 300 square acres. But the Paradise boundaries have been extended through Jesus Christ. There is no difference between Jews and Gentiles in these New Testament times. The boundaries of the Garden of Eden have been extended to the uttermost parts of the earth. The system of salvation was established so that those who believe can enter heaven. Outside of salvation, there is only everlasting fire, the same thing intended for all of the fallen angels.

The Bible says that everyone who has sinned comes under the wrath of God. This is why Jesus is so important in our lives. He is the only one who can bring us to God and allow us to live eternally with Him. Salvation is a gift given to mankind, that is, if they believe and accept the Son of God as their Savior. Jesus tasted death for everyone; He died for us all. Jesus was the propitiation for the sins of the whole world.

Doom and devastation came to this world through the first Adam, but justification came to this world through the last Adam, Jesus Christ.

"This mystery is that through the gospel the Gentiles are heirs together with Israel, members together of one body, and sharers together in the promise in Christ Jesus" (Ephesians 3:6, NIV).

In Old Testament times, circumcision and salvation was available to only Jews. They were the saints who entered into the righteous part of Sheol. But now, there is no difference between Jews and Gentiles. Gentiles are fellow heirs with Jews in the blessings of salvation and grace. The Garden was extended to the entire world through the church. The Garden of Eden had a limited space, but the entire world now has a chance to make the Garden their heritance by obeying the laws of God. Those who confess Jesus Christ as their Lord and Savior and believe in their hearts that God raised Him from the dead shall be heirs to the kingdom of God (Romans 10:9-10).

The promise of God is extended to every human being on earth. This is the gospel we, the Victory Prayer Center, have been preaching to our people for the last sixteen years. Three churches have been established—two are in villages—and many souls who were in terrible darkness are now coming to the light of Christ.

Once, we went to a hill village called Vanthada. We climbed three hills in order to reach these hill people. There, we found fifty families. The entire land was only about fifty acres. We preached to them by going hut to hut. They heard the gospel and we prayed for them. I have never forgotten that experience. It gave me the satisfaction that I bore a tiny part of the cross my Lord carried in the streets of Jerusalem. Let us all together carry the cross to reach the unreached in these last days. Let us preach the gospel again to the materialistic world, which has been backsliding from the love of Christ.

CHAPTER -10

PARADISE REVEALED

Did Jesus Mention Paradise in His Teachings?

This is very difficult question to answer. Jesus did not mention paradise directly but when we meditate on the teachings of Jesus Christ, we can see that in the scriptures, He answered the Pharisees and Sadducees in Matthew19:3-5, ASV: "And there came unto him Pharisees, trying him, and saying, Is it lawful for a man to put away his wife for every cause? And he answered and said, Have ye not read, that he who made them from the beginning made them male and female, and said, For this cause shall a man leave his father and mother, and shall cleave to his wife; and the two shall become one flesh?"

Jesus knew every detail of the creation of the universe and the creation of man and woman. God the Son supported the view that man and woman were created by God as per the Genesis account. I marvel at the people who believe in the evolution theory and how faith in God is diminishing in the hearts of the people. If evolution is 100 percent correct, then why are we seeing amoebas the size of a human palm in the deep oceans? This does not support evolution.

In the book of Matthew, Jesus talked about the days of Noah, how the people behaved, and prophesied about the end times. "For as in those days which were before the flood they were eating and drinking, marrying and giving in marriage, until the day that Noah entered into the ark, and they knew not until the flood came, and took them all away; so shall be the coming of the Son of man" (Matthew 24:38-39, ASV).

Many people did not believe Noah and doubted the global deluge. But it was real and the evidence for this incident was discovered recently by scientists. This generation seems to be weak in their faith in God, possibly because of their materialistic attitude. "And without faith it is impossible to be well-pleasing unto him; for he that cometh to God must believe that he is, and that he is a rewarder of them that seek after him. By faith Noah, being warned of God concerning things not seen as yet, moved with godly fear, prepared an ark to the saving of his house; through which he condemned the world, and became heir of the righteousness which is according to faith" (Hebrews 11:6-7, ASV).

Faith is the medium, or tool, to reach God. We cannot prove God by the laws of this world. He is beyond our every imagination. If human beings invented infinite ways to solve a great problem on this earth, God will be able to solve that same problem in yet other way.

Jesus talked about the lost Paradise in Matthew 24:28, which has been a mystery to the Christian Church. In my regular Bible reading, every year when I came to this verse, I would marvel at the words used by Jesus in this sentence: "Wheresoever the carcase is, there will the eagles be gathered together" (Matthew 24:28, ASV).

Why did Jesus use the above sentence while prophesying about the end times in Matthew 24? I used to ask the Lord, "Lord, if it is your will to reveal the meaning of this sentence to me, please reveal it." After several years, the Spirit of God led me to know the meaning of this sentence. Here, we should know that carcass is a negative word, and even Jesus did not call the body of Lazarus a carcass. At that time, Lazarus' body was wrapped with clothes and he lay down like a carcass. He was dead for four days. "When Jesus therefore saw her weeping, and the Jews also weeping who came with her, he groaned in the spirit, and was troubled, and said, Where have ye laid him?" (John 11:33–34, ASV, underlined for emphasis).

So the word carcass in this chapter has its own meaning. Jesus never used any sentence as a proverb or any sentence without specific meaning. The above sentence has great meaning.

When we see the shape of the Dead Sea, we marvel at it. The Dead Sea is like a carcass (dead body) facing east. So carcass is nothing but the Dead Sea. Thank God for this revelation. This may help us to understand other scriptures in the right way.

If we examine world history, we will come to know that eagles are the insignia of many countries and armies. Jesus referred to eagles when He spoke to His disciples. In Luke 17:37, ASV, we read: "And they answering say unto him, Where, Lord? And he said unto them, Where the body is, thither will the eagles also be gathered together." Let us observe some examples given below:

- In 102 BC, a Roman ruler by the name of Gaius Marius decreed that eagles must be the insignia of their senate.

- Persia (present-day Iran) uses an eagle as its military sign.

- In 20 BC, Herod the Great, who constructed the second temple, used an eagle as an insignia on the main entrance, which the Jews objected. Consequently, the sign was removed.

- In the twelfth century, an Arab ruler by the name of Saladin used an eagle as his country's insignia with the words "Saladin Golden Eagle." After that, many Arab countries used this insignia in different ways.

Countries That Have Used an Eagle as an Insignia:

1. Egypt, Iran
2. Many countries in Europe AD 1871
3. On Roman coins between AD 1172 and AD 1192
4. Germany in the fifteenth century

5. Poland, Austria, Albania, and Russia
6. America

Prophetically, we must understand that eagles stand for the world kingdoms. We cannot say whether America will indulge in a military campaign or not, but Israel will surly become a cup of intoxication. So all Christians should observe the developments in Israel and other countries and continue their spiritual journeys, preparing themselves for His soon coming. Eagles (kingdoms) gathering together against Israel is not a new thing, but we see a pointer to a particular place in Matthew 24:28.

In Daniel 5:22-23, we see how Belshazzar, son of Nebuchadnezzar, defiles the holy vessels by using them to drink wine. He also worshipped gods made of brass, iron, wood, and stone and tasted the wrath of God. Even in these days of knowledge explosion, should we not pray for people with spiritual blindness who do not understand that their bodies are temples of the living God? In Proverbs 24:11, NIV, it is says, "Rescue those being led away to death, hold back those staggering towards slaughter."

In these end times, God wants everybody to repent and be baptized. Otherwise, they will have to stand on the left side with those who are condemned for hell. They will have to hear God's harsh words as mentioned in Matthew 25:41, NIV: "then he will say to those on his left, depart from me, you who are cursed, into the eternal fire prepared for the devil and his angels."

Let us now study a small thing the Lord uttered in Matthew 24:2, NIV: "Do you see all these things?' He asked, 'I tell you the truth, not one stone here will be left on another, every one will be thrown down.'"

The Lord prophesied these words at approximately in AD 27. In AD 70 Nero, a Roman emperor, attacked Jerusalem through his army general, Titus, and burned the city. In this attack, the gold in the Sanctum sanctorum of the temple melted and spread between the stones of the temple. So to salvage that gold from among the stones, the Roman soldiers moved every stone of the Temple for the extraction of melted gold on the stones. Thus, all the prophecies of Jesus were exactly fulfilled at different times. Similarly, the prophecy that says, "Where there is a dead body, there the eagles will gather" will also be fulfilled.

The Gathering of Eagles in the Past

Let us now consider an incidence where eagles (world kingdoms) gathered in Israel. After Israel was formed on May 14, 1948, Arabs all around became her natural enemies. In May 1967, Abdul Nazer, the president of Egypt, vowed to wipe out Israel from the world map by destroying the entire nation. About 900 million Arab soldiers surrounded Israel, which had merely 2.2 million soldiers. The countries that attacked Israel were Egypt, Syria, Jordan, Saudi Arabia, and Iraq with open support from Russia. It was estimated that they got ready for· this military campaign with arms and ammunition worth 300 million dollars. But stunning the whole world, Israel defeated them with the help of Almighty God who "neither sleeps nor slumbers." During this six-day war, all the eagles (kingdoms) were not gathered at the carcass. So it was not supported in Jesus' prophecy in Matthew 24:28. I believe it will be fulfilled in future. In Matthew 24:30, it is mentioned that at a time when the eagles (world kingdoms) gather at the carcass (the Dead Sea). These days, we read in newspapers that Iran is acquiring technological know-how to prepare weapons of mass destruction and trying to get the necessary uranium from Russia to make atom bombs to destroy Israel. We also see how the eagles from the European Union (EU) are going to join the eagles in the Arab countries against Israel in the near future. As the redemption of the church is going to take place at the same time, let us lift our heads and look up. In Revelation 22:7, NIV, the Lord says, "Behold, I am coming soon! Blessed is he who keeps the words of the prophecy in this book."

The revelation that God has given to John is being fulfilled in these days. The meaning of this prophetic utterance, "where there is a dead body, there the eagles will gather" in Luke 17:37 has been hidden in the past but is now revealed in the present. Before coming to the conclusion that eagles signify the nations around Israel, I referred to Preaching through the Bible-Matthew by

Michael Eaton, a leading Bible teacher. This man of God has compared and concluded that the "eagles" in Matthew 24:28 are the world kingdoms. Praise the Lord!

Even the world, which is so valuable in the sight of man, is simply like a dead sea without the living waters of Jesus. This present generation is fully saturated with worldliness and without salvation (living waters) they are like the Dead Sea. For this wealth, there is a possibility of the world kingdoms gathering together. Eagles rush toward a carcass to feed on it. In the same way, the world kingdoms may vie each other for the chemicals and minerals of the Dead Sea. In the sight of God, the Dead Sea is a valley that has hurt God's heart and now stands as a symbol of man's disobedience. This is the very place where the people of Sodom and Gomorrah were burnt with fire and brimstone. In the sight of God, the world without salvation is equivalent to a carcass (Ephesians 2:1).

But in the sight of the world, this Dead Sea is going to be very valuable in the future because there is a possibility of all the world kingdoms gathering there. The Lord likened the prepared church to be His bride. That is why the value of the church in the sight of God is very great. Such a valuable church must adorn herself with impeccable holiness. Only such a church will be invited for the royal banquet.

This thought is reflected in Revelation 19:7, NIV: "Let us rejoice and be glad and give him glory! For the wedding of the Lamb has come, and his bride has made herself ready." So every believer must prepare himself or herself without expecting somebody to prepare them.

As the Dead Sea is a part of Israel and this country has been the focal point of human history, it will continue to be the focal point of future human history. Let us watch the developments in Israel and compare them with scriptures to prepare ourselves for His second coming. May God give insight into the prophecies given to the church in these end times.

Jesus Mentioned Paradise on the Cross

In Luke 23:43, NIV, we can read the powerful statement of Jesus regarding Paradise: "Jesus answered him, 'Truly I tell you, today you will be with me in paradise." The thief on the cross believed that the crucified Jesus would reign on the earth. He admitted that Jesus was the prophesied Messiah and that He had already established His spiritual kingdom on earth. It was a great message to the unbelieving Jews and the priests. The eyes of the high priests should have been opened by this great statement of the thief on the cross. I observed that all the parallel translations used the word paradise about this verse.

The word paradise has Persian origin and has a meaning of "garden," which gives pleasure and rest. A garden certainly consists of fruit-bearing trees, a joyful atmosphere, and it will be a place of rest. The OT saints always talked about a paradise that was inside the earth, a living place (Sheol) of the dead. Jacob said to his sons with tears in Genesis: "But Jacob said, 'My son shall not go down with you; for his brother is dead, and he alone is left. If harm should befall him on the journey you are taking, then you will bring my gray hair down to Sheol in sorrow" (Genesis 42:38, ASV, underlined for emphasis).

The patriarch of Jewish people revealed the truth about the Paradise inside the earth, referred to as Abraham's bosom (Luke 16:22-23). Many believe that place was the righteous part of Sheol. From this verse, we can understand that Paradise was transferred to Sheol during the Flood and in turn, it was shifted to the third heaven after the crucifixion of Jesus Christ. The multipurpose plan of God through the cross of Jesus Christ is evident at this point. Jesus' soul went down to Paradise (righteous part of Sheol), and He brought back the captives, freeing them from bondage. The souls had been arrested by the enemy in Sheol. We know that from the Lazarus and rich man's story, there was a gulf between unrighteous and righteous part of Sheol.

Why were the righteous people of the Old Testament held captive under the authority of darkness? Because the penalty for the sin of Adam was not yet paid. A righteous God never deviates from His own heavenly law and all truth is parallel. His only begotten Son came over this world and paid the penalty. Because of Adam's disobedience, the sin was passed down from Adam through the souls of the Old Testament saints.

In Sheol, He never left the righteous souls, and God gave a refuse, or resting place, which was the bosom of Abraham who was the father of the people who believed in God.

Abraham's bosom was under the authority of darkness and they were in complete rest. That captivity was carried away by the power of the blood of Jesus Christ. The devil lost this battle. This was a devastating loss for Satan, never to be regained. What a wonderful victory we received through the blood of Jesus Christ who became our redeemer! We can read this in Luke 4:18- the mission statement of Jesus Christ.

The cross of Jesus Christ brought forth the following gifts to the past, present, and future generations:

- Salvation through faith in Jesus
- Deliverance to the OT saints who were resting in the righteous part of Sheol
- Shifting Paradise to the third heaven along with the OT saints, including the thief on the cross
- Spiritual kingdom has been spreading through the church system and the physical kingdom will appear on the earth very soon! Get ready.
- The death on the cross and resurrection on the third day changed the worship day from Sabbath

> to Sunday (according to the New Testament order we found in Acts and other epistles)

The Dead Sea was the gateway to shift Paradise to the third heaven. You may ask, "How was that possible? How did the trees survive inside the earth? How was the carbon dioxide supplied to the trees in Paradise inside the earth?" I do not know all these things. According to the scriptures, I simply believe the above facts.

Everything is possible with God. The Old Testament saints talked about Sheol under the earth. But the New Testament saints talked about Paradise in the third heaven. Dear Reader, we can understand the link between the OT and NT statements. Paul was writing his own experience about his soul going into the third heaven. If it is difficult to believe that Paradise could be inside the earth, it is also not possible to believe Paul's testimony about his voyage to the third heaven. If it is wrong, everything should be wrong. Yet it is not. Paul was bold enough to declare, "Be ye imitators of me, even as I also am of Christ" (1 Corinthians 11:1, ASV). So Paul supported the idea of Paradise in the third heaven.

Paradise is an abode for souls and the language of Paradise is mysterious. Every Christian knows that the church (bride) will catch up to the third heaven for a seven-year feast. I am waiting for it. This is the hope of Christianity.

The Holy Bible mentions Paradise from Genesis to Revelation. The revelator, John the apostle, mentioned Paradise when he was exhorting to the church in Ephesus: "He that hath an ear, let him hear what the Spirit saith to the churches. To him that overcometh, to him will I give to eat of the tree of life, which is in the Paradise of God" (Revelation 2:7, ASV).

The Tree of Life is mentioned in many books of the Bible and Paradise is mentioned as well. Paradise is the place where the Creator came and fellowshipped with His precious creation—man and woman. This place was hidden for many thousands of years, and it was revealed to the church so that we can proclaim that Bible stories are not myth; there is evidence for every biblical incident that has occurred upon the face of the earth. Many of us are well acquainted with the news of Noah's Ark hidden under the snow upon Mount Ararat. The global flood has been a problem for many scientists; many cannot agree as to whether it was global or local. Noah's story was real, the Flood was global, and the entire Bible is true. I believe the stories of the Bible without the need of evidence. "Verily I say unto you, Whosoever shall not receive the kingdom of God as a little child, he shall in no wise enter therein" (Luke 18:17, ASV).

So the Paradise mentioned in the book of Genesis was not lost or deteriorated like the things made by mortal human beings. The Garden of Eden was planted by Almighty God, so it could never be lost.

As I wrote in the previous chapter, the Garden was recovered, shifted, and restored for the habitation of righteous souls. Let us believe it unconditionally and occupy it by grace through the cross of Jesus Christ. "O the depth of the riches both of the wisdom and the knowledge of God! how unsearchable are his judgments, and his ways past tracing out! For who hath known the mind of the Lord? or who hath been his counsellor?" (Romans 11:33-34, ASV).

We should not try to teach God. God Himself planned the Garden, restored the Garden, and with His wisdom He sent forth the fallen angels to the pit through the Flood. While manifesting this great deluge on earth, the deepest point on the earth—the Dead Sea-was formed in the actual location of the Garden of Eden. May God bless everyone who believes this truth. Get ready for His coming!

TESTIMONY

I am the third son of Pastor Rjaratnam and Mrs. Jeevaratnam. My father came from a Hindu family. He married a pastor's daughter and got saved. While he was trying to find work, God directed him to go to Bible school. He obeyed. He completed his Bible studies and then started a ministry in the Madupalli village where I was brought up.

Being brought up as a normal Christian boy, I listened to the Word of God quite a bit. There were annual Christian conferences in my grandfather's town and it was at one of those meetings that I got saved. It was 1982. In that same year, God spoke to me through the scriptures: "But now thus saith Jehovah that created thee, O Jacob, and he that formed thee, O Israel: Fear not, for I have redeemed thee; I have called thee by thy name, thou art mine. When thou passest through the waters, I will be with thee; and through the rivers, they shall not overflow thee: when thou walkest through the fire, thou shalt not be burned, neither shall the flame kindle upon thee. For I am Jehovah thy God, the Holy One of Israel, thy Saviour; I have given Egypt as thy ransom, Ethiopia and Seba in thy stead. Since thou hast been precious in my sight, and honorable, and I have loved thee; therefore will I give men in thy stead, and peoples instead of thy life" (Isaiah 43:1–4, ASV).

I have since completed my pre-university course in Ramachandrapuram, a town in Andhra Pradesh. I was awarded a bachelor's degree in mathematics at PR Government College at Kakinada, which is affiliated with Andhra University, Visakhapatam. During this time, I had attended a church that had a great burden for lost souls. Then the seed of evangelism was planted. I want to be a faithful servant to my Lord, and so I started my career as a mathematics teacher. During that time, I supported local church pastors.

In 1990, I married a beautiful woman named Vijaya Kumari, who was the daughter of a pastor who was working in Orissa, North India. I used to read and meditate on one chapter each morning. One day, my father-in-law gave me a book called Bible Pathway. It was a guide to complete the Bible in one year. I read through it fourteen times (that is, three chapters in thirty minutes, and I completed the Bible fourteen times in fourteen years). It was a wonderful experience; my soul was being filled with the Word of God. I have been blessed with three children: my daughter, Jyothi Threressa; my son, Jessie Hemanth; and my other son, Samuel Sumanth.

While I was working as a math teacher, I felt the Lord lead me to where I currently live. I started my own ministry by founding a church in 1997 named Victory Prayer Center.

God promised in Isaiah 42:1-6, ASV: "Behold, my servant, whom I uphold; my chosen, in whom my soul delighteth: I have put my Spirit upon him; he will bring forth justice to the Gentiles. He will not cry, nor lift up his voice, nor cause it to be heard in the street. A bruised reed will he not break, and a dimly burning wick will he not quench: he will bring forth justice in truth. He will not fail nor be discouraged, till he have set justice in the earth; and the isles shall wait for his law. Thus saith God Jehovah, he that created the heavens, and stretched them forth; he that spread abroad the earth and that which cometh out of it; he that giveth breath unto the people upon it, and spirit to them that walk therein: I, Jehovah, have called thee in righteousness, and will hold thy hand, and will keep thee, and give thee for a covenant of the people, for a light of the Gentiles;"

6 Dr. John A. Hash, Ed. Bible Pathway, compiled from Bible Pathway Devotional Guide (Tennessee: Bible Pathway Ministries, 1999).

As I continued my ministry in Samalkot, an opportunity opened up for me to complete a Master of Divinity course by the Asian Theological Academy in Bangalore.

Many souls are being saved through our church ministry. My name and address were put on a mailing list from Sovereign World Trust. They have been kind enough to support me by sending valuable literature in order to improve my knowledge of the Bible. I congratulate the supporters of SWT. They send valuable books to pastors, like me, who live in Third World countries.

Again, God spoke to me through scripture: "Call unto me, and I will answer thee, and will show thee great things, and difficult, which thou knowest not" (Jeremiah 33:3, ASV).

I am continuing His ministry by extending my ministry to two more villages. I believe God is standing with me and performing many miracles in my ministry. We have completed the church building in Samalkot (our mission center), and we are trying to construct more churches in other villages where we are working.

Suddenly, in 2008, I lost my dear son, Samuel Sumanth, to leukemia at the age of eleven. I was in deep darkness and I felt as if there was no hope in my life. So I prayed to God. "God, I want to quit the ministry, and I want Your permission to do so. Please show me three people who can lead the churches I started." As I prayed, God told me, "I want you to write a book about the revelation you asked of Me." I was still waiting on the Lord to give me permission to leave the ministry. I did not get that permission. So I obeyed God and said, "Yes Lord, I want to complete my course in this world. Let me complete my work on this earth." God then comforted my wife and He filled us with more grace.

We have many plans to reach the unreached in India. Please pray for my ministry. God gave me a plan to preach the gospel in these remote villages that are being neglected. I support other pastors who are working in villages where there is opposition, and as a team, we go to villages to preach the gospel to the poor. We wish to help pastors who are facing financial troubles in building their churches.

How God Led Me to Write this Book

"But you are cast out, away from your grave, like a loathed branch, clothed with the slain, those pierced by the sword, who go down to the stones of the pit, like a dead body trampled underfoot." (Isaiah 14:9, ESV).

Oh! What a wonderful revelation of a "carcass" trodden underfoot. The word trodden means "trampled" or "crushed" underfoot. These words give us the meaning of pushing and pressing down. This is nothing but the Dead Sea in Israel, so I have collected information and maps explaining how the "carcass" was formed, the meaning of the above verse, and the meaning of the scriptures in Ezekiel 26:19-21, 28:8-19, and Ezekiel 31.

So when I got the revelation about "Paradise," which was lost during the Flood, I immediately started to plan the publication of this book. I strongly believe that those who know the Bible very well can understand this book and along with my next title: End- Times @ Dead Sea. This book, Paradise Found, was not written with mere human knowledge, but it is the revelation of God given to remove the uncertainty about Paradise, which was lost.

It was revealed to me by the Spirit of God. Before reading my words, I request every reader to go through the scriptures given in that context. Human knowledge cannot perceive these truths.

The Bible says, "But unto us God revealed them through the Spirit: for the Spirit searcheth all things, yea, the deep things of God. For who among men knoweth the things of a man, save the spirit of the man, which is in him? even so the things of God none knoweth, save the Spirit of God. But we received, not the spirit of the world, but the spirit which is from God; that we might know the things that were freely given to us of God. Which things also we speak, not in words which man's wisdom teacheth, but which the Spirit teacheth; combining spiritual things with spiritual words" (1 Corinthians 2:10-13, ASV).

116

The bottom line is that everything possible with God. Jesus revealed this mystery to the babes in this world. I never thought of writing books. I have spent much time understanding the correct interpretation of the scriptures, because I believe the Bible is the source of answers to every uncertainty. It is a treasure of secrets and mysteries. It is like a well-anybody can draw out living waters, with the help of the Spirit of God. The Bible is interpreted by itself, not by any other source.

Jesus said, "At that season Jesus answered and said, I thank thee, O Father, Lord of heaven and earth, that thou didst hide these things from the wise and understanding, and didst reveal them unto babes: yea, Father, for so it was well-pleasing in thy sight. All things have been delivered unto me of my Father: and no one knoweth the Son, save the Father; neither doth any know the Father, save the Son, and he to whomsoever the Son willeth to reveal him" (Matthew 11:25-27, ASV).

I have searched the entire Bible to learn more about the Garden of Eden and how it was removed from the earth. I know that the Garden of Eden was a real place and that it was not mythological. In my research, I realized that the remnant of the Garden of Eden is at the Dead Sea.

So when I got the revelation about Paradise, which was lost during the Flood, I immediately started planning to write a book.

I am giving this book for the edification of the church worldwide and to reveal the deep and hidden meaning of the scriptures. Read it and if you feel it is worth reading, introduce it to your church and friends. May God bless you abundantly and prepare us for the extension of His kingdom in these last days.

My church, Victory Prayer Center, is involved with many ministries

Present

- LIFE (Love India Festival Evangelism) crusades

ministries:
- Bible school
- Book ministry

Planning to start

- TV ministry
- Mass LIFE festivals in major cities
- Victory Christian Library
- Supporting village evangelists and pastors
- Samuel Sumanth Memorial Trust (helping poor children in their education)

We would greatly appreciate your love, prayers, and support to help us keep these ministries going and to continue to move into more towns and villages in India.

With much love, we thank you!
Yours in His service,
Anipe Steeven K. V. Premajyothi, B.Sc; B.Ed; M.Div.
Author, Paradise Found
D. No: 1-3-49/1, Victory Compound
Pension Line
SAMALKOT-533440
EG DT AP INDIA.
Mobile: 9493050992 ,8074871493
Email: victorprem.vpc@gmail.com.

BIBLIOGRAPHY

Duffield, Guy P. and Nathaniel M. Van Cleave. Foundations of Pentecostal Theology. Charisma Media, 1983.

Eaton, Michael. Preaching through the Bible: Genesis 1–11. Tennessee: Sovereign World Trust, 1997.

Paradise Lost----A Simplified Summary, Book by Book. Paradise Lost Study Guide. New Arts Library. 1999,

All Rights Reserved,
http://www.paradiselost.org/novel.html; Internet accessed 15 August 2011.

ACKNOWLEDGMENTS

I thank my mom and my wife for their prayers and encouragement

to write this book.

I appreciate my congregation for their prayers for the success of this book.

I bless my daughter, Theressa, and son, Hemanth, for their help in proofreading and typing.

I thank members of the BlueRose Publishing team for their help and friendly approach at every stage of preparing and publishing this book. May God bless every reader of this book.

BOOKS PUBLISHED

Eye of the Sahara @ Plate Tectonics

How fascinating it is to think about the geological wonders of the earth. During the 1960s, the Richat Structure, or Eye of the Sahara, unexpectedly came to light thanks to astronauts. This discovery led to many speculations and assumptions about this structure. This book answers the misconceptions about the formation of the Eye of the Sahara. According to this book's hypothesis, in 1405 BC (on Joshua's Long Day), major geological changes occurred in the North Atlantic Ocean, and Atlantis was submerged in the Atlantic Ocean by tectonic plate movements of the Earth. During this submersion, the junctions of the South and North American tectonic plates with the African and Eurasian plates opened wide, and lava and melted magma, about 100 Giga Pascals of pressure, erupted from the Inner Earth like an ICBM (Intercontinental Ballistic Missile) and poured upon a spot in Mauritania, creating the geological wonder known as the Eye of the Sahara. Go through the book and certainly marvel at this.

Joshua's Long Day @ American Tectonic Plate Movements

A prominent 3rd Century (BC) Philosopher narrated the story of Atlantis and used a phrase' it was destroyed in single day and night'. When the author was searching for physical evidence on earth for the miracle of Joshua's Long day, this phrase became a base in the space of historical speculations about this occurrence. It is not possible to be missed a continent in a single day and night. It was only possible with tectonic plate movements in the Atlantic Ocean:

- There was a link between Atlantis deluge and Joshua's Long day.
- Atlantis was deluged by tectonic plate movements in Atlantic Ocean.
- Central American region was at navigable distance to Atlantis prior to 1405 BC.
- North & South American Plates diverged and Nazca and cocoos plates sub ducted.

- Sea Floor spreading was occurred in mid Atlantic ridge.
- African and Arabian plates stand stood for about a day i.e Joshua's Long Day.
- American Plates travelled with unusual speed – terrible tsunamis and earthquakes hit the land of Atlantis and around Mediterranean Sea.
- There were many long day and long night (other side) occurrences recorded.

Above points discussed in detail in this book. The people of Atlantis belonged to Bronze age . Many evidences given to support this view. Many books and researches of noble persons helped to come to a comfortable conclusion Atlantis Deluge @ American Tectonic Plate Movements.

This book is available in amazon and flipkart.

Yours
Anipe Steeven King VPJ B.Sc; B.Ed; M.Div
Author, Paradise Found
Email: victorprem.vpc@gamil.com,
918074871493

PF ENDORSEMENTS

Paradise 'Garden of Eden' lost due to the sin and disobedience of first Adam. This was a big loss to the entire human race. This Paradise was missed from the earth and history. This was a hidden mystery from the beginning. There is an answer for every problem in the Bible. Where was the Garden of Eden? This was the challenging issue to every Christian and non-Christian. The prominent 17 century poet narrated the story of 'Paradise Lost' through his poetry. But we do not know actual location of the Paradise.

God revealed this mystery to his servant and the Paradise was Found in Israel itself. Are you wish to know the location of the "Garden of Eden" on the face of the earth?. Please come with me by reading the God revealed truth about lost Paradise which was Garden of Eden, then you can found it on the earth geographically and also you will agree with me. Praise the Lord, the Paradise was Found. Those who lost the Paradise in their hearts, please read this book diligently, you can restore it by the Spirit of God.

" But thou art cast forth away from thy sepulcher like an abominable branch, clothed with the slain, that are thrust through with the sword, that go down to the stones of the pit; as a dead body trodden under foot." Isaiah 14:19 (ASV).

Dead body mentioned in this scriptures is nothing but ' Dead Sea'. This was proved through this book.

As mentioned in the above scriptures Isaiah 14: 19 Lord God trampled the fallen spirits into the pit through the Garden of Eden region during the Flood. All the details given through the graphics and maps you can easily understand this revelation. If you find difficulty in your first reading , please go one more round . I believe that the Spirit of God help you to understand this book . Please post your opinion about this book .

- Jesus asked Simon Peter to go deep into the sea to cast his net for a catch (Luke 5:4). Similarly PastorAnipe was inspired to cast his net of innovative mind to find out the lost Paradise. In this connection, I would like to quote below a few lines from a famous hymn:

> " Thy word is like deep,deep mine,
> And jewels rich and rare,
> Are hidden in mighty depth
> For every search there."

May God bless his work and his ministry.

- Anipe's book 'Paradise Found' makes an interesting reading. It entails historical facts which are at once absorbing and fascinating. It is not simply the outcome of intellectual exercise but a brain child of divine revelation. It not only speaks volumes of the authors extraordinary interest in Biblical themes, but also his untiring efforts to fathom the unknown

- Anipe'sbook , really, is a revelation from God, the Almighty . The author has delved deep into very interesting facts in Biblical history. He has taken an untrodden path of biblical research to find out the exact location of Garden of Eden. May God bless him.

--Rev. Elijah Sade
Pastor, Indian Pentecostal Church, Attabira

www.ingramcontent.com/pod-product-compliance
Lightning Source LLC
LaVergne TN
LVHW061615070526
838199LV00078B/7288